THE PARDON

AND

OTHER

STORIES

MARK BURTON

Printed in the United States of America
ISBN 1-931232-69-5

Xulon Press
11350 Random Hills Road
Suite 800
Fairfax, VA 22030
(703) 279-6511
XulonPress.com

CONTENTS

The Pardon.....1

The Promotion.....15

The Present.....27

The Promise.....39

The Pageant.....55

The Pitch.....67

The Pilgrimage.....77

Partiality.....107

THE PARDON

"What does this mean?" Sammy asked.

"It means you're home free, dummy," Donny said.

"Shut up," Sammy replied, hitting Donny in the chest with the back of his hand.

Sammy's public defender looked rather somber despite the legal victory. She had wanted to defend the innocent poor and knew that to do so she would sometimes have to defend the guilty poor, like Sammy. The pardon, however, was too much even for her 15 years' worth of cynicism. "It's a full pardon by the President."

"You mean *the* President?" Sammy asked.

"It's some sort of election year thing," the lawyer said. "I think it's...."

"What?" Sammy asked.

"I think it's ridiculous," the lawyer said. "They must have made a mistake. This pardon is worded for both the past and the future."

"But it's still good, right?" Sammy asked.

"Oh, it's good," the lawyer said. "Good for you and good for everyone else who got one."

"So what's this stuff about the future?" Donny asked.

"You've not only been pardoned for all of your past crimes," the lawyer told Sammy, "but you've been pardoned for all of your future crimes, as well."

"Are you kiddin' me?" Sammy asked.

"That's the way it's worded," the lawyer said. "When the press hears about this, I'm sure it will backfire in the President's face. But he signed it, so it's legally valid."

Sammy held the piece of paper in his hand as if reading it over, but the legalese made no sense to him.

"Man, you know what you've got?" Donny said, the excitement growing in his voice. "What you've got there is a genuine get-out-of-jail free card."

"Is that right?" Sammy asked the lawyer.

She hated telling him. She had sized Sammy and his buddy up a few days before, when she was assigned to Sammy's case. She knew from the paperwork that Sammy was 28, but he acted as if he were just out of high school. To her, it was clear that these were just two lazy white guys whose main goal in life seemed to be avoiding responsibility. Still, she did not really know Sammy and, despite his seemingly trivial arrest record, she was afraid that he might go on a crime spree. The thought even occurred to her that she might be his first "legal" victim. For the moment, however, she was still his court-appointed attorney and was obligated to explain the pardon. "Yeah, that's right. You can still get arrested, but all you have to do is show the pardon and they'll have to let you go."

"I don't believe it," Sammy said.

"Congratulations, Sammy," the lawyer said. "You're a free man. A very free man. Now if you'll excuse me, I have other clients to see."

"Thanks," Sammy said, extending his hand. "Thanks a lot."

"It wasn't my idea," the lawyer said, refusing to shake.

After she walked away, Donny turned to his friend. "Man, Sammy, this is great! What do you want to do first?"

"I don't know," Sammy said. "Celebrate, I guess."

"Yeah, yeah, let's celebrate," Donny said, following Sammy across the courthouse lobby like a puppy dog after its master.

* * * * *

It was past midnight when Sammy crushed the last can of the six-pack.

"Remember when we used to drink back here in high school?" Donny asked.

"Yeah," Sammy said. "Seems like a long time ago."

"Yeah," Donny agreed. "This shopping center was practically brand new back then."

"The trash dumpsters still smell the same," Sammy said, sniffing the air.

"Well, for a man with a get-out-of-jail free card, you've been mighty quiet," Donny said. "Let's try it out."

"I don't know, man," Sammy said. "I read this thing twice and I can't figure it out. What if she was lying?"

"She can't lie to her own client," Donny argued. "She has to tell you the truth."

"So what am I gonna do?" Sammy asked.

Donny thought for a moment. "Do something simple. Something that won't matter much if you get caught."

Sammy eyed Donny with a mischievous look. "You know what I've always wanted to do?"

"What?" Donny asked.

"You know when the lights turn red all in a row out on the strip?" Sammy began. "Well, I've always wanted to see if I could run every light before one of them turns green again."

"Hey, man, go for it," Donny said. "There's no traffic this time of night."

"Okay," Sammy said, putting his keys in the ignition. "Let's do it."

Sammy pulled out of the shopping center and positioned his car at the first stop light, straddling both lanes. The light was green, but he did not go.

"Anybody coming?" Sammy asked.

"Nope," Donny said, sticking his head out of the window. "I don't hear anything, either."

The light turned red, but Sammy still waited. As soon as the lights at the next five intersections had turned red, Sammy floored it. They made it through all six red lights and kept going.

"Yeah!" Sammy shouted, giving Donny a high-five with this right hand.

"Oh crap," Donny said out of habit as soon as he heard the siren.

Sammy pulled over and checked the rearview. "County cop."

"Get the pardon out," Donny said, suddenly nervous.

As the officer approached, Sammy rolled down his window. "Evening."

"Good morning," the officer said. "Do you know why I pulled you over?"

"Because I just ran six red lights?" Sammy assumed.

The officer paused for a moment. "No, actually I pulled you for doing 48 in a 35, unless there's something you'd like to confess."

"No sir," Sammy said. "You're right, I was speeding. I'm sorry."

"Can I see your license and registration, please?" the officer requested.

Sammy struggled to get his wallet out of his back pocket while Donny fumbled through the glove compartment. Donny passed the pardon letter to Sammy along with the registration.

"What's this?" the officer asked, eyeing the pardon.

"I just got it today," Sammy said. "It's a pardon from the President."

"Yeah, right," the officer cracked.

"I'm serious," Sammy said. "Check it out. It was on the news and everything."

The officer walked back to his patrol car and stayed there for about 20 minutes talking to his dispatcher.

"Why is it taking so long?" Donny asked.

"I guess he's checking it out," Sammy said.

"Maybe you shouldn't have given it to him," Donny said. "What if he just tears it up?"

"He can't do that," Sammy said. "Besides, they got copies on record down at the courthouse."

After a few more minutes, the officer came back.

"Smells to me like you fellas have had a few beers," he said. "Now, you might not mind endangering your own lives, but there are other people on the road, too."

"It checked out, didn't it?" Sammy asked.

The officer paused, then returned Sammy's paperwork. "Yes, it checked out, but…."

"So I'm free to go," Sammy said, cutting him off.

"Yes, you're free to go," the officer answered reluctantly.

"Well thank you, officer, and enjoy the rest of your shift," Sammy said, starting his engine.

"Yeah, buddy!" Donny yelled after they had pulled away.

Sammy's adrenaline was pumping. "It's real. It's really real."

"We gotta do something else," Donny said.

"I don't know, it's getting kinda late," Sammy said, calming down a little.

"Come on," Donny pleaded. "We gotta do something else. How about Mrs. Crutchins' cat?"

"What?" Sammy asked.

"Let's do something to her cat," Donny said. "Like we always planned back in school."

"That cat's probably dead by now," Sammy said.

"Maybe…" Donny said.

Sammy and Donny grinned at each other.

"Okay," Sammy agreed, remembering those beer-buzzed nights when he and Donny would ride around with Donny's father's .22 looking for cats to shoot.

"Stop by my place," Donny said. "I got my rifle in my trunk."

* * * * *

"Just drive by first," Sammy said.

They had left Sammy's car at Donny's house. They had agreed that Donny would drive his car and Sammy would do the shooting.

"You know how to load it?" Donny asked, a bit protective of the .22 he had inherited.

"Yes, I know how to load it," Sammy retorted as he filled the magazine.

"Here it is," Donny said as they approached Mrs. Crutchins' house. She had a large corner lot in the old neighborhood where Sammy and Donny had grown up. Two overgrown bushes protected the front steps, where the sidewalk met the front porch. A street light illuminated the intersection, but her house was set back far enough that the trees kept it in the shadows.

"See anything?" Donny said, slowing the car to a crawl.

"Nah," Sammy said, making sure to keep the rifle below window level in case someone was watching them. "Go around again."

Donny circled the block once more, then stopped in the middle of the street directly in front of their target's house.

"Don't stop here," Sammy protested. "Pull it over to the curb, up there."

Donny pulled it over about halfway between Mrs. Crutchins' house and her neighbor's house. He cut his lights but left the engine idling.

"I thought I saw something on the porch," Sammy said. "Wait here, and keep it running."

"Okay," Donny said.

Sammy looked up and down the block to make sure no one was around, then he exited the car as quietly as he could. He carried the rifle almost vertically, close to his right leg, and tried to look casual as he walked across Mrs. Crutchins' lawn. When he got to the sidewalk, he could see a cat lounging on the porch. He looked around again and, seeing no one, he raised the rifle, aimed at the cat and fired.

It was only a .22, one of the smallest caliber rifles made, but the noise from the shot still startled him so much that he ran toward the house and hid behind the large bush near the front steps. He waited, expecting the entire neighborhood to wake up, but after a minute or so it was clear that no one was going to check out the noise from the shot. He was too close to Mrs. Crutchins' house, however, to see the light that had come on in one of the upstairs rooms. Then he heard the cat. It was not dead. It was only wounded. It lay on the porch, making a low, guttural sound. From the corner of his eye, Sammy noticed that Donny was waving to him to get back in the car. Sammy motioned with his left hand for Donny to wait.

Moving around the bush, Sammy approached the steps and saw the cat. One more shot, he thought, would put it out of its misery. He put one foot on the lower step and raised the gun to fire again. Before he could fire, though, the front door opened and Mrs. Crutchins stepped out, dressed in a house coat. She moved slowly and appeared to have a hard time seeing. Sammy was surprised at how old she looked.

"What's the matter, huh?" she said as she opened the front screen door and saw the cat lying there, almost growling. "What's wrong with you?" She was talking to the cat and had not even noticed Sammy.

Sammy lowered the rifle from his cheek, but did not notice that he still had it pointing in the general direction of Mrs. Crutchins. The movement, however, caught her eye. When she looked up and saw Sammy with the gun, she gasped.

"No," Mrs. Crutchins said under her breath.

"What?" Sammy asked, still standing in the same spot and still holding the gun.

"Please don't," Mrs. Crutchins pleaded.

"Hey, I'm sorry," Sammy told her. "I was just…I don't know, I just…."

What do you say to a little old lady, he thought, when you've just shot her cat? He could think of nothing. He noticed, however, that tears were now streaming down Mrs. Crutchins' face.

"Take anything," she said, her voice trembling. "Take the car, if you want. I don't use it much anyway, not anymore."

"I'm not going to rob you," Sammy said, surprised that she would think that.

His words seemed to frighten her even more. "Please…" she begged. "Please don't hurt me."

It was only then that Sammy noticed he still had the gun pointed at her. He quickly pointed it away. Slowly, he began to realize that she had not recognized him; that she did not understand why he was there; that she thought she was begging for her life.

"I'm not going to hurt you," he said. "I just wanted to shoot your cat."

As soon as he uttered the words he knew just how stupid they sounded. He lowered his shoulders, turned his head and sighed in frustration. Then he looked again at Mrs. Crutchins. She was kneeling, one hand still holding the screen door open and the other one shaking, barely touching the cat. Her eyes were filled with tears and Sammy could not tell if she believed him. When the cat's heavy panting suddenly stopped, she looked down.

"Oh, my poor baby," she cried softly. She looked down at the cat and gently stroked her hand across its back.

"I'm sorry," Sammy said, almost whispering. When Mrs. Crutchins did not look up again, he turned and went back to the car.

* * * * *

After they had driven out of the neighborhood, Donny pulled into the parking lot of a strip shopping center and cut the engine.

"Are you gonna say anything or not?" Donny asked.

"She thought I was going to kill her," Sammy said.

"What'd she say when she saw the cat?" Donny asked.

"She thought I was going to kill her," Sammy said again, much more forcefully. "She really thought that I was going to kill her."

"Okay, okay," Donny said. "So what's the big deal? Did she recognize you or something?"

"No, I don't think she recognized me," Sammy said.

"Hey, man," Donny said, tapping Sammy's arm and trying to lighten the mood, "even if she did recognize you, what's she gonna do? Have you arrested?"

Donny tried to laugh but Sammy would not join in.

"What is wrong with you?" Donny asked, desperate to change the mood. "You know what? I know what you need. You need some whiskey shots. Remember that party we went to, and you were doing all those shots? How many was it? It was like, six in a row or something, wasn't it? I never seen you that wild before or since."

"I lost my job because of that," Sammy said. "I was sick that whole week."

"That construction job?" Donny said. "That was no big deal. Construction jobs come and go, man."

"My Dad had set that up," Sammy said. "He was friends with the owner. I could've worked for that company the rest of my life."

Donny turned his head and looked out the window. His attempt to change the subject and relive the good old days had failed, so now he would switch to his back up plan. He would pretend to be offended because Sammy was not behaving the way a drinking buddy should. The tactic had worked before.

"I don't get you, man," Donny said, turning back to Sammy. "I just want us to have a good time, and you're always bringing me down."

"Don't start, Donny," Sammy said. "This is different."

"What's different?" Donny asked. "What are you talking about?"

"What I did back there was wrong," Sammy said.

Donny ridiculed the idea by making a sound with his lips. "Pffp. You picked a stupid time to start caring."

"It's not stupid," Sammy said. "You didn't see the way she looked at me. I'm not a murderer."

"It's stupid because you don't have to worry about it anymore," Donny said loudly and slowly. "You can do whatever you want. You've got the pardon, remember?"

"Let's just call it a night," Sammy suggested after a pause.

"I don't want to call it a night," Donny said. "I want to get something to drink."

"Okay," Sammy said, "but drop me off on the way."

"No," Donny said. "We're right where we need to be. There's the liquor store."

"Then get something and let's go," Sammy said.

Donny looked at Sammy and rolled his tongue in his cheek.

"What?" Sammy asked.

"I don't want to pay for it," Donny said.

Then Sammy realized what Donny had done.

"You pulled in here on purpose, didn't you?" Sammy complained. "You were planning to rob that store all along."

"No," Donny said coolly. "I was planning for *you* to rob it."

"No way," Sammy said.

"Look," Donny rationalized. "We're here. We've got the gun. Just do it."

"Since when did we become liquor store bandits?" Sammy protested.

"Since you got that pardon," Donny retorted.

Sammy fell back against the seat and looked up at the ceiling of the car.

"Donny, listen to me," Sammy said. "I've been thinking about this all afternoon, and that stuff with Mrs. Crutchins just brought it all home. I know you think this pardon sounds like a free pass do whatever I want, but I don't. I just don't feel that way. The way I see it, someone must have looked at me and said 'this guy's worth a second chance.' And you know what? I am. I am worth a second chance. I don't want to be some punk for the rest of my life. I don't want to rob liquor stores. I just want to do what's right. And I never, ever want to shoot another cat for as long as I live."

They both grinned a bit at Sammy's last sentence. With the tension broken, Donny decided to ease up a bit.

"I was just joking about the store," Donny lied. "But you gotta admit, it's kinda tempting. Right?"

"Yeah, I'm tempted," Sammy said, grabbing the pardon from the top of the dashboard. "But this pardon…I don't know. I don't know how to explain it. It's like, part of me is still tempted to do all that stuff, but now it's like I've suddenly got this better half or something. And the better half knows that all that stuff is wrong. I used to get a kick outta breaking the rules, breaking the law every now and then. But now, with this pardon, the law doesn't matter. There are no more rules. Not for me, anyway."

"Let me see if I've got this straight," Donny said. "You

used to like breaking the law, but now that you're allowed to break the law, you don't want to anymore?"

"What if I had killed Mrs. Crutchins instead of her cat?" Sammy asked rhetorically. "According to the law, there's a really big difference between killing a cat and killing a person. But when I killed that old woman's cat, I must have broken her heart just as if I had shot a bullet through it. The pardon made me realize that what's wrong is wrong."

"Oh, give me a break," Donny complained.

"I know it sounds corny," Sammy said, "but try to understand. Before today, I didn't mind doing minor stuff because even the law said that some crimes were trivial. But with the pardon, killing Mrs. Crutchins' cat is pretty much the same as killing Mrs. Crutchins. I don't go to jail either way. So now I've got to decide whether or not I want to be a murderer, because now I can, if that's what I really want. Well, I know that I do not want to be a murderer. But since killing the cat is the same as killing a person, it means that I don't want to be a cat killer, either."

"You're losing me, man," Donny said, shaking his head and rolling his eyes.

"Look at it this way," Sammy tried again. "The law tries to list all of the bad things a person could do, and it says that some crimes are worse than others, so some punishments are harsher than others. With the pardon, I'm free of all that crime and punishment stuff. All I have to worry about now is what kind of person I want to be. Whoever decided to give me that pardon must have known, somehow, that I want to be a good person."

"And all good people run six red lights in a row whenever the opportunity comes along," Donny argued.

"I told you," Sammy replied, "I'm still tempted. Running

the lights was a mistake. I shouldn't have done it. But now I feel bad about it. Before I got the pardon, I don't think I would've felt bad about it. Before, I only felt bad if I got caught."

"And you feel bad because now you realize that running a red light is the same as murdering Mrs. Crutchins?" Donny asked sarcastically.

"No," Sammy answered, exasperated.

"So what now?" Donny asked. "You gonna turn into some goodie two shoes or something?"

"I don't know about that," Sammy said. "The difference, I guess, is that, in the past, doing the wrong thing was my heart's desire. Only the fear of getting caught held me back. Now, it's almost the opposite. Now my heart's desire is to do what's right. I'll still make mistakes, but I want my heart to be in the right place."

"Your heart's desire?" Donny mimicked. "Did you get a job writing greeting cards and forget to tell me?"

"Cut me some slack," Sammy said.

"All right, all right," Donny caved. "I guess that cat thing really messed you up. I'm sorry I suggested it. Okay?"

"Okay," Sammy agreed.

Donny started the engine and drove out of the lot, thinking that things would be back to normal the next day. Sammy, however, knew that their long, ignoble friendship was over.

THE END

THE

PROMOTION

It was either late summer or early fall and Mary and Jim Buckley were taking their usual after-dinner stroll around the neighborhood. Their shadows stretched before them on the sidewalk as they headed down the nameless side street that separated their subdivision from the last remaining farmland in the area.

Across the street, the creak of the Williams' cellar door briefly caught Mary's attention as the two young Williams boys and a friend raced up and out of the basement and into the backyard. When the last boy let the cellar door slam shut, the noise seemed to cue the ever-plump Mrs. Williams, who was inside cooking supper.

"I told you, you can play inside or out, but not both," Mrs. Williams yelled from the kitchen window of the old farm house. "Now what's it gonna be?"

Ten-year-old Curtis consulted with his friend while his younger brother Eddie could only wait. "Inside," Curtis responded shortly, and the two older boys headed in through the back screen door with Eddie bringing up the rear.

Meanwhile, Mary and Jim had maintained a straight course and were now about half a block from the T-intersection with Old Barn Road. It was a two-laner that used to meander through the countryside past cornfields and old Victorians. Now it was mostly a shortcut for hurried commuters trying to avoid traffic lights.

One of those Victorians—the one with two grand oaks that shaded the intersection until about noon each day—belonged to Mr. Gerald "Gerry" Berry, who had bought the house after retiring early. Jim had heard that by the time Berry and his late wife had fixed the place up the way they wanted it, ground had been broken for the first subdivision of split-levels. Except for a few old farmhouses, like Mrs. Williams', the rolling hills of corn, fields and woods had long since been replaced by cul-de-sacs and cheap siding.

Mary and Jim were the third couple to buy in that first development, and they eventually developed a friendship with Mr. Berry after joining the same Baptist church that he had joined upon retiring. Mr. Berry had once told Jim that he felt somehow cheated out of the peaceful retirement that he had planned—cheated by the so-called progress that had turned the countryside into a stale regurgitation of the older suburb that he had worked so hard to escape. Now Mr. Berry was 83 and, although he seemed as feisty as ever, he could only make it to services on Christmas Eve and Easter morning. Mary and Jim made it a point to walk past his house during their strolls and often stopped to chat if they saw him sitting on his front porch.

They still had a few minutes before they would reach Mr. Berry's house, so Jim decided to spring some news during a lull in the conversation. "I, uh…I got it," he said, looking down and almost biting his tongue.

"What?" Mary asked.

He did not speak but, unable to suppress his pride any longer, he turned his head toward Mary and smiled that one-cheek smile of his.

"You got the promotion?" she asked excitedly.

Jim nodded. They stopped walking and turned to each other, both of them grinning beyond control. Mary let out a big sigh. "I knew you'd get it," she proclaimed. She put her arm around his back and they resumed their walk.

The smiles faded a bit and Jim became more serious. "I guess it's too little too late."

"No, honey," Mary said. "With Tammy out of college now, we can use the extra money to save for those retirement years. And maybe a new car. And maybe new cabinets for the kitchen. And maybe we could close off the porch and make it a sun room. And…."

"Ahem. I think we should stick to just saving for a while," Jim interrupted, knowing full well that she was pulling his chain. "Besides, I have a sneaking suspicion we might need a new roof sooner than later."

"Hmm," Mary scowled at the thought, knowing that her husband was probably right.

They were now at the end of the sidewalk, at the intersection with Old Barn Road. On the other side of the road, Mr. Berry was sitting on his porch, looking sort of like he did the day that Jim had first met him, except that now the chair beside him was empty. He waved that old man's wave when he saw them and his loneliness pushed him out of his chair, even though he didn't feel like getting up.

"Don't get up," Mary shouted as she and Jim crossed the

road. They met about halfway up Mr. Berry's front walk. "You're looking good," she said.

"I'm still here," Mr. Berry said. "I guess ya'll are walking twice around tonight?"

"I'm sorry?" Jim asked.

"I say I guess you'll have to walk around two times tonight, since it rained last night," Mr. Berry explained.

"Oh, oh," Mary and Jim responded out of synch. "Well, I don't know about that," Mary said.

Mr. Berry waved across the street and when Mary and Jim turned to look they saw Mrs. Williams getting her mail and newspaper. "Hello, Mrs. Williams," Jim said on behalf of the group.

"Hello," Mrs. Williams responded, making her way across the road. "Hello," she said again, crossing the shallow grass ditch that, except for the occasional drunk, separated Mr. Berry's lawn from the traffic. "Not much traffic today," she noted.

"No. I'm surprised," Mary added.

"I don't like all that traffic," said Mr. Berry. "They always speed up and down here."

"Oh, I know," Mrs. Williams agreed. "I'm always telling the boys to stay away from that road."

"How's everything going?" Mary asked.

"It's going, I guess," Mrs. Williams said.

"You still working that other job?" Mr. Berry asked out loud what Mary was thinking.

Mary and Jim did not know Mrs. Williams very well, but they remembered the night the ambulance came when Mr. Williams had the heart attack. Mrs. Williams usually worked swings as a nurse at the hospital and was not home when it happened. One weekend, about a month after the funeral,

Mary and Jim stopped for lunch at Pete's Place and Mrs. Williams waited on them.

"Yes, and now they want all the waitresses to bus tables, too. I tell you right now, I'm too old for that," Mrs. Williams laughed.

"I know you work hard. I see you. I see you leave every morning," Mr. Berry said. "You didn't know this old man got up that early, did you? Well I do. Every morning."

"Oh, I bet you do, Mr. Berry, I bet you do," Mrs. Williams replied.

* * * * *

Upstairs in the boys' bedroom, Curtis and Eddie watched as their friend pulled a worn book of matches from his front jeans pocket.

"You got any cigarettes?" the friend asked, trying to be cool.

"No," Curtis said.

"How about some paper?" the friend asked.

"What kind of paper?" Curtis asked.

"You know—something we can burn," the friend said.

Curtis was about to decline, but then Eddie spoke up. "You better not," Eddie said.

Now Curtis was on the spot. He knew what his mom had said, but he could not acquiesce to a command from his younger brother, especially in front of his friend.

"Here," Curtis said, pulling two sheets of Eddie's crayon doodles from a pile beneath the bed and handing them to his friend.

Eddie stood up. "I'm tellin'," he threatened.

"You better not," Curtis said, echoing his younger

brother's words on purpose.

Eddie called for his mom but there was no answer. He called again, and again no answer. The friend went to the window.

"She's outside," the friend noted, mouthing the words silently to Curtis so that Eddie would not understand.

Eddie was not sure what to do, so he just watched as the friend returned from the window and struck the first match. The paper burned easily, and soon the friend was lighting the second sheet with the first. As the flames grew larger, Eddie became increasingly worried, until finally he ran out of the room, calling for his mother.

* * * * *

Back in Mr. Berry's yard, the conversation was still centered on Mrs. Williams' hardships. "...and the stove died yesterday," she said. "I never liked camping the way Fred did, but I'm glad I kept his old gas stove—that's how I'm cooking supper tonight."

They all smiled, politely but genuinely, yet Jim did not understand why. It was not so much what Mrs. Williams had said, but the way in which she spoke, that seemed to imply humor of some sort, despite the gravity of the subject matter. Maybe it was a "black" thing, he thought.

It was then that Curtis and his friend came running across the yard and across the road.

"Mama," Curtis started, a little out of breath.

"What did I tell you about crossing that road?" Mrs. Williams said sternly.

"Mama, don't get mad..." Curtis tried again.

"Then next time you better stop and look both ways," she

continued.

"No, Mama, not that," Curtis said. "The house…I mean… there's a fire. The house is on fire."

The adults were briefly stunned. They spent about one second looking at Curtis, expecting more details, then they looked over at the house, which appeared to be fine.

"Mr. Berry, can I use your phone?" Mary asked.

"Yes, go," Mr. Berry said. "You know where it is, right?"

Mary nodded and headed for Mr. Berry's front door. As she did, Jim and Mrs. Williams started toward the house.

"You stay here with Mr. Berry," Mrs. Williams told Curtis. Then it hit her. "Where's Eddie?" she asked.

Curtis had forgotten about Eddie. He tried to explain, but his open mouth would not produce the words. His friend cowered off to the side, looking up from a lowered head with deceptively innocent eyes.

"Oh no," Mrs. Williams said, starting across the road.

"No," Jim said. "I'll get him. Curtis, where is he?"

"I think he's upstairs," Curtis replied, responding to the deepness and authority of Jim's voice.

Jim trotted across the road. He noticed smoke filtering through the screen of a second-floor window. He went in through the front door. A hallway led straight back through the center of the house. The living room was on the left, and stairs leading upward were to the right of the foyer area.

"Eddie?" Jim called. He did not hear an answer, so he went upstairs. Smoke was rolling along the upstairs ceiling, pouring out of a bedroom door. "Eddie?" he called again at the top of the stairs. Still no answer. He checked the bathroom at the end of the hall, and then the main bedroom, both of which seemed relatively clear of smoke. He knew he had to go into the room that was on fire, but the heat was already making him sweat. “Eddie?” he called from the hallway, squinting through the doorway at what appeared to be an inferno engulfing the bed.

He heard nothing but the growing roar of the fire, and saw no one. “Eddie?” he tried to go in, but the heat and the smoke were too great. Then he saw that the closet door was ajar. “Eddie?” he shouted as loudly as he could. He had to check. He then ran back to the bathroom, soaked a bath towel with water, and returned to the bedroom doorway. Holding the wet towel over his head and back with both hands, he dashed into the room and over to the closet, kicking the closet door open with his foot.

He used one hand to push aside the hanging clothes, but the closet was so small he could tell right away that no one was in there. By the time he ran back out of the room, the towel was smoking. He had to crouch to keep his head out the thickest layers of smoke, which by then were billowing ferociously.

He went back downstairs and was surprised to see that smoke now filled the entire house. Then he peered into the small living room and saw that the fire had already started to burn through the ceiling. He did not see anyone, so he went down the hallway toward the kitchen and the back room, which had been Mr. Williams’ den in years past.

* * * * *

“I called the fire department,” Mary said as she emerged from the house.

“It must have been that old propane tank,” Mrs. Williams speculated. “Oh, Eddie.”

“I wish we had 9-1-1,” Mary said. “I had to call the

operator."

"I'm sorry. I put the emergency numbers by the bedroom phone," Mr. Berry responded. "Just never got around to...."

"That's all right, Gerry," Mary reassured him.

The wail of sirens seemed faint until the first truck thundered over the crest in the road and pulled onto the Williams' front lawn. Two firemen hurried to the hydrant near the intersection just as a red EMS unit arrived.

"You two stay with Mr. Berry," Mrs. Williams told the boys. "You hear me?"

"Yes, ma'am," Curtis responded.

Mrs. Williams started across the road. Mary followed, glancing back at Mr. Berry, who made a pushing motion with his hand for her to go ahead.

"My son's inside," Mrs. Williams shouted, hurrying toward the nearest firefighter—a young blonde woman just getting out of the cab. "My son's inside. And there's a man in there, too."

"My husband went in to get the boy," Mary explained.

"John, two people inside," the firefighter shouted to a fireman who was putting on a helmet, mask and tank. He acknowledged with one big nod and a thumbs-up.

An attendant from the EMS unit moved Mary and Mrs. Williams farther from the house and away from the trucks.

"Where are they?" Mary asked, referring to her husband and Eddie.

Mrs. Williams just shook her head. All they could do was watch. By now a third, larger truck had arrived. An older man had gotten off and seemed to be taking charge. The smaller truck had focused a hose on the second floor bedroom window, which was now gushing thick, heavy smoke.

The fireman in the special gear grabbed an ax and headed

to the front door. The man in charge did not notice until another fireman ran up to him and said something in his ear. The man in charge turned and shouted "No, absolutely not," but it was too late. The front door was ajar and the fireman in the special gear was nowhere to be seen. The man in charge threw his helmet to the ground in a move of controlled frustration.

Another hose from the larger truck was directed onto the roof. About a minute after the fireman had gone in, a small explosion blew out the side window of the kitchen. Mary and Mrs. Williams heard it, but could not see what was happening because they were almost on the opposite side of the house. When the fireman in the special gear emerged from the front door, Mrs. Williams took a few steps toward the house but was intercepted by an EMS attendant. Mary stayed back.

The fireman pulled his helmet and mask off and waited on the stoop while the man in charge and another fireman trotted up to him. Mary could not hear what was being said, but she grew weak when she saw the fireman lower his helmet and slowly shake his head back and forth.

Mrs. Williams saw it, too, and she began to panic. "No, Eddie, not my Eddie." It took both EMS attendants to hold her back and she nearly collapsed on the ground.

Mary did not know what to do. For a brief moment, she wondered why she stood frozen while Mrs. Williams was screaming and thrashing about in a fit of anguish. She could think of only one thing to do. With eyes closed she bowed her head, clasped her hands and prayed a silent prayer.

The firefighters, meanwhile, were beginning to get the blaze under control, but the smoke continued to rise upward in a twisting column high above Mary and the house. And on the other side of the rising smoke, down below in the back yard, the setting sun was casting shadows, two of which were on the sidewalk, holding hands, not far from the now open cellar door.

THE END

THE PRESENT

Josh Rucker tried to be quiet as he one-handed his house keys. He had just painted the porch last weekend, but the boards were at least as old as he was and creaked with every shift of his weight. Despite the noise, he was glad that the bolt was thrown on the front door. It meant that his wife, Susan, had gone on to bed rather than wait up. It was the first night in weeks—since he had started moonlighting at the grocery store—that she would not be up to greet him.

Once inside, he locked the door behind him and proceeded to the kitchen in stealth mode, hanging his jacket on the back of his kitchen table chair. As he mixed himself a glass of chocolate milk, he realized that he missed having Susan greet him at the door. He finished his milk, rinsed the glass out in the sink, and headed down the hallway. He paused in front of his daughter's room. Her door was slightly ajar and he pushed it open just enough to see that she was sleeping soundly. He had wanted his first to be a son, and still wanted one, but it never ceased to amaze him just how wonderful having a daughter had turned out.

Josh slipped into the master bedroom and started to undress. Susan rustled and eventually turned on her night stand lamp.

"Sorry, honey," Josh whispered.

"I don't think I was asleep, anyway," she responded. "I set the alarm for seven."

"Oh, yeah," Josh sighed, remembering his pledge not to let work interfere with church.

* * * * *

A few hours later, not too long before dawn, a man was loading a truck in back of an old strip shopping center on the other side of town. An old department store, unused for the previous two years or so, had been purchased by a discount chain. The new owners had hired the man to remove as much of the junk and debris from inside the store as he could. The man surveyed the inside one last time before pulling down and padlocking the loading dock door. He walked around the back of his truck to check the load and noticed that there was one more box of metal scraps that he had missed. There wasn't much room, but he managed to squeeze the box on because he wanted this trip to be the last haul of the night.

His truck was one of those older-style, two-axle commercial flatbeds, with four wheels on the back axle, wooden slats on each side of the bed and no tailgate. He had picked it up used about ten years earlier, shortly after he started moonlighting as an odd job man. Despite the bad shocks and no AC, it had served him well.

As he turned onto Prince Street, he noticed that all of the lights were green. He knew from experience that if he missed just one, he would get out of synch and would have to stop at all of them, so he accelerated just a bit after making the first light. He hit a bad pot hole, but he figured that it was unlikely the front end could get any worse. So he drove on, making every light, never noticing that the box of scrap metal had fallen off.

* * * * *

The next morning, Josh woke up to the sounds of spring—mostly the chirping birds that had made a nest in the tree outside the bedroom window—and the smell of breakfast cooking in a skillet. He stumbled into the kitchen.

"I thought we were on a diet," he asked.

"We'll make an exception on Sundays. And Saturday nights, too, apparently," Susan said with a smile, holding up the chocolate milk glass that still had the spoon in it.

"It's not my fault, Your Honor. It's society's fault for making the stuff in the first place," Josh joked.

Without intending to, his joking reminded both of them of his younger days, his drinking days, when chocolate syrup was the last thing he would use for a mixed drink.

"Never again," he said somberly.

"I know," she assured him. "Why don't you go shower now so I can get in after we eat?"

"Okay," he said, and down the hall he went. "Mary? It's time to get up. Get up and get ready for church."

"I'm up, I'm up, I'm UP!" Mary answered.

"Okay okay OKAY!" her daddy yelled from his bathroom.

Before long they had finished their bacon and toast and

OJ and half of a cinnamon toaster tart for you-know-who. Susan told Mary to put on something nice for church while she took a shower and Josh went outside to get the paper.

It was a surprisingly fresh morning, with only a few wisps of clouds and a slight breeze that still had a bit of left-over winter in it. Josh decided to cruise the yard while he waited on the women. He was halfway around the house when he saw Mary struggling to exit the back door. She had dressed up all right—in her cowgirl outfit, complete with hat, denim skirt, plastic pistols, holsters, and a cumbersome broom-handle horse that apparently had a thing about screen doors.

"Has Mom seen you yet?" Josh asked.

"Not yet," she said, coming down the steps and mounting up.

"I didn't think so," Josh said. "I'm not sure they'll let cowgirls take their guns into church."

"I'm not a cowgirl," she retorted, galloping around a bit. "I'm the sheriff, and I have to have my guns."

"Why?" he asked.

"To shoot the bad guys," she answered as she came to a stop on the sidewalk. "Like this." She drew and fired two imaginary shots at her Dad, making a shooting noise each time. "Pi-choo. Pi-choo."

"Oh, you got me," Josh exclaimed, clutching his abdomen. He "fell" slowly to the ground and then laid motionless on the grass.

Mary expected him to get up, but grew concerned after about 30 seconds. She dismounted and walked over to her Dad, whose eyes were shut tightly in a bad bit of acting.

"Daaaad," she said.

Josh slowly opened his left eye wider and wider, turning

his head away from her and his eye toward her at the same time in an almost clownish fashion. He raised his left arm and she grabbed it, helping to pull him up.

"You know you should never point a gun at anyone unless you're in real danger," he said.

"But it's not a real gun," she contested.

"It doesn't make any difference," he said in his fatherly-advice tone of voice. "You don't point guns at people, whether they're real guns or not, whether they're loaded or not."

"What about bad guys?" she asked.

"Right now you don't have to worry about bad guys."

"All right you two," Susan called from the door. "What's going on?"

"Just a little horse play," Josh said, picking up Mr. Horsey and directing Mary inside. "Here, put Mr. Horsey back in your room and put the guns away, too. And the hat."

"But I wanna wear the hat," Mary complained.

"You can wear the hat in the car, but you have to take it off when we get to the church," Susan compromised.

"Okay," Mary reluctantly agreed.

"And you, Mr. Rucker," Susan said as her husband came through the door. "You've got grass stains all over your good shirt."

"Oops. I'll change," Josh said.

"No, we don't have time. Just keep your sport coat on."

"Honey, I'll burn up," Josh protested. "You know how warm it gets in there."

"Maybe they've turned the heat off by now," she said.

"I don't know..." Josh moaned.

* * * * *

Mrs. Wellstone was driving to her mother-in-law's that morning, with her toddler safely tucked in the child's seat in the back of her new sedan. Actually, Mrs. Wellstone and her husband had purchased the car jointly, but he had graciously offered to drive the old pickup until they could afford the next new car. She was glad and somewhat surprised that her husband had agreed both to get the car she wanted and to let her drive it. She still did not quite understand, however, what he had meant about trading this year's first round pick for a future option.

She did not see the metal debris in the road, but she knew right away when the tire blew. She had suffered her first flat on the last car, and there was no mistaking it this time. She pulled off near a gravel parking lot and got out to inspect the damage.

* * * * *

The Ruckers arrived at the church with about 15 minutes to spare, but there were no more parking spaces in the regular lot. Josh dropped Susan and Mary off and then headed toward the overflow lot at the end of the block, opposite the T-intersection with Prince Street. He did not like crossing Prince at that spot because there was no light there and the traffic was usually fast and heavy through that stretch. When he saw a car on the other side blocking the Prince Street entrance, he was forced to turn onto Prince, then into the alley—a more circuitous but safer route that allowed him to enter the lot through the side entrance. Getting out of his car, he noticed that the vehicle blocking the Prince Street entrance had a flat. A slightly pudgy woman in a dress and overcoat was trying to change the right rear tire.

"Ma'am, can I call a tow truck for you?" Josh asked.

"No, thank you," Mrs. Wellstone replied, her little girl swaying beside her, staring at Josh with a partially-clad Barbie doll firmly in her grip. "I gave up and called my husband."

Josh returned the lady's chuckle with a smile and figured everything was okay. He looked both ways and, seeing that the traffic was still caught at the light, trotted across the road. But then he heard the lady shout.

"Becky!"

Josh turned and saw Mrs. Wellstone still on the other side of the car, but the toddler had moved around to the front of the car and started to cross the street, apparently following Josh. And the light had changed.

Josh ran back into the street and scooped up the little girl. Out of the corner of his eye, he kept watch on the cars at the light as they started to move. It was the vehicle coming from the other direction that he did not see. It hit him so hard it knocked the toddler out of his arms even before he fell to the pavement.

Mrs. Wellstone rushed into the street and was relieved to find Becky crying but unhurt. Then she pulled her cell phone from her coat pocket and started to dial.

* * * * *

Just inside the main church doors, Susan was talking with the Wrights while she waited for Josh. The Wrights were an elderly couple that had been friends of Josh's parents before they died. Mary was just outside, running around on the church's grassy front lawn.

"I *thought* that was Josh," Mrs. Wright said.

"He's hoping that he can stop after he gets his first promotion," Susan said. "We're both hoping, actually."

"It's a shame his father isn't around to see him now," Mr. Wright said. "After all that trouble."

"Ed…" Mrs. Wright intervened.

"That's okay," Susan assured her. "Mary, get off the ground. Come here."

Mary had started to roll around on the grass, but obeyed her Mom's orders without hesitation. As she approached, Susan took her by the arm and started brushing her off.

"Hello, Mary," Mrs. Wright said.

"Hello," Mary responded.

"Hi Mary. You ready for Sunday school?" Mr. Wright asked.

"I guess so," Mary answered.

"She's just like her father," Susan said. "This morning I caught *him* rolling around in the grass. He got grass stains all over his Sunday shirt."

"He wears the same shirt every Sunday?" Mrs. Wright inquired.

"What's wrong with that?" Mr. Wright asked as Susan nodded in response to the shirt question. "Why, I've worn this same suit to church every Sunday for…oh, I'd have to say five years now."

"More like ten," Mrs. Wright said, leaning forward to direct her comment to Susan.

"Okay, maybe ten," Mr. Wright acknowledged. "But it just goes to show you, Mary, if you take care of your property it will last a long, long time."

"Ten years is a really, *really* long time," Mary added, and they all laughed.

It was then that the squeal of tires caught their attention.

Susan was standing near the doorway and had the best view. When she saw people start to run toward the overflow lot, she began to get worried.

"Will you watch Mary?" she asked the Wrights. "I want to go see what happened."

"Certainly," Mrs. Wright said.

Just after Susan walked out a siren began to wail in the distance. As it grew louder, Mrs. Wright gave her husband a concerned look.

* * * * *

The lawn of the church extended to Prince Street, with a row of mature oaks and elms lining either side. The grass was still wet from a short predawn sprinkle, so Susan decided to take the sidewalk. She saw a crowd gathering at the intersection and she quickened her pace when she noticed the siren growing louder. A ring of people had formed around someone lying facedown in the street, and there were a couple of cars off to the side.

"Does anyone know CPR?" she heard a voice say as she made her way to the center of the ring. No one responded to the call. And then she saw him.

The people standing around sensed that she knew him and let her through. Though she wanted to shout it, she could not even whisper his name. She placed her hand on his back, afraid to roll him over.

"All right, stand back, stand back," a police officer commanded as he guided the medical technicians through the crowd. The ambulance had parked on the church lawn because there were too many people and cars blocking access to the scene. The police officer put his hands on

Susan's shoulders and moved her aside while the two med techs knelt down on either side of Josh, facing each other.

"What hit him?" one of the techs asked as they made preliminary observations. No one answered out loud, but most of the people in the crowd looked toward a white trash truck that, until then, had sat relatively unnoticed just beyond the ring of people. "Well," the tech said to his partner under his breath, "at least it wasn't the kind with the fork lifts on the front."

* * * * *

The Wrights and Mary were standing in the front doorway of the church, wondering with many others in the congregation what the commotion was all about. A high school boy approached, slightly out of breath. "A member of the church got hit by a bus or something," he said. "I think someone should get the pastor."

With that, the boy went inside with a few others. The Wrights decided to follow some of the other congregation members who had started toward the accident scene. They marched hurriedly down the lawn in staggered formation, most of them somewhat embarrassed by their morbid curiosity, but all of them genuinely concerned that one of their own might be in trouble.

When they got to the end of the lawn, they saw the ambulance parked on the grass with its back doors open and a man on a stretcher being rolled toward it. Leaving a path for the stretcher, the crowd from the church and the crowd from the intersection merged into a wide semicircle behind the ambulance. Almost instinctively, the church members began to drop to their knees and pray silently as the stretcher went past. Even old Mr. Wright dropped one knee into a muddy patch of sod, oblivious that he was bringing his ten-year streak to an end.

The two med techs had never seen a crowd respond that way. They glanced at each other almost nervously as their progression continued to cause a domino-like cascade through the crowd. Susan and a couple of police officers followed the stretcher until they got to the ambulance, where the med techs paused to lower the stretcher.

Mary, who had remained standing beside Mr. Wright, walked toward her mother as soon as she saw her, but she ended up at the foot of the stretcher by coincidence. It was at that moment that everything seemed to come together for the crowd and the med techs. The tearful woman being held back by the officer was the hurt man's wife, they realized, and the confused little girl, obviously their daughter, was about to find out that her daddy was seriously injured.

Susan saw Mary and ran to comfort her before she turned to see who was on the stretcher. She knelt beside her daughter and stroked her hair, but she knew that it might be the last time Mary would see her father. She looked up at the med techs, and they knew that she wanted them to wait a moment before loading the stretcher into the ambulance.

Then Susan looked at Mary, and looked at the stretcher, indicating that Mary should look, too.

When Mary turned and saw her daddy lying there, motionless, she thought about the incident in the yard earlier that morning, but she sensed that this was different. She stepped closer, to the side of the stretcher, watching, waiting, hoping for her father to open his eyes. And the crowd watched, and Susan watched, and the med techs and police officers watched, all hoping for the same thing.

Just as Mary was about to give up, about to turn back to her mother, she noticed some movement. Slowly, her father opened his left eye and, straining against the neck brace and the pain of his injuries, he raised his left hand toward his daughter. Mary stepped closer and grabbed his hand with both of hers. He gave one squeeze, then closed his eyes and lowered his hand back down.

Susan moved forward and put her arm around Mary, while the med techs put the stretcher in the ambulance. And back at the church, as if looking down on the entire scene, a chrome-plated cross on the pinnacle of the steeple shimmered in the bright morning sun.

THE END

THE

PROMISE

Joe Davidson had left work early. He strolled through the open-air market that late afternoon, thankful for the breeze coming in off the water. At first he was surprised that the place was so busy on a September weekday, but then he remembered that it was Friday and school had just let out.

As he strolled down the hill toward the marina, with skateboarding teenagers whizzing past and day-trippers walking their bikes up, he heard someone ringing a ship's bell. The bell ringer was inside a large ticket booth for charter fishing boats. The sign indicated that charters left every hour on the hour. The bell was apparently the five-minute warning for the four o'clock departure.

Davidson was interested, but a review of the prices posted on the side of the booth made him reconsider. He walked on, admiring the yachts and sailboats bobbing comfortably in their slips. Then he noticed an older woman and a small girl boarding a boat. A handcrafted wooden placard nailed to a piling advertised ten-dollar mini-cruises.

"Do you have room for one more?" Davidson asked as he approached.

"Uh, I don't know," said James, a summer-hire ship's mate. "Let me ask the Captain."

"I think we can handle one more," Captain Peters said as he emerged from the small storage area within the bow. "No fishing, though. Just sightseeing."

"That's fine with me," Davidson replied, handing James a ten-dollar bill.

Davidson boarded, silently refusing the help offered by James. Davidson estimated that the boat was more than 10 or 15 years old and more than 20 feet long. It had an inboard engine below deck, allowing plenty of room in the open-air aft. The cockpit was covered by a hard-shell top and there was enough room in the forward hold for one or two people to lie down. It appeared to Davidson that the boat was just a family pleasure craft and he assumed that the "captain" was probably a retired landlubber trying to make a few extra bucks. For only ten dollars, he figured he could live with it.

Once they were underway and clear of the one drawbridge between the marina and open water, Captain Peters let James take over as helmsman. He spun around in the swivel chair opposite James and introduced himself.

"I'm Frank Peters," he said, "but my friends all call me Captain." He paused, frowning at the staid response from his passengers. "Hey, c'mon, I usually get at least a snicker out of that."

Davidson did not get it, but extended his hand and broke the awkward silence. "I'm Joe Davidson."

"I'm Helen Simpson," the older woman said, "and this is my granddaughter Eileen."

"Do ya'll live around here?" the Captain asked.

"Yes," Davidson answered. "I live about 30 minutes up the road. Thought I'd start the weekend early."

"Uh-huh, uh-huh," the Captain nodded. "And what about you, Eileen? Are you from around these parts?"

"No," she said reservedly.

"I live in town," Mrs. Simpson added. "Eileen and her parents are visiting."

"Have you ever been on a boat before?" the Captain asked Eileen, trying to get her to come out of her shell.

"No," she said.

Sensing the girl's reluctance, the Captain decided it was a good chance to say a little bit about himself, as he usually did on each excursion. "Well, I have," he started. "I fished these waters for 28 years. Not just fish, neither. Crabs, shrimp, oysters. Just about everything, I guess."

"Why do your friends call you Captain?" Davidson asked.

"Well, I'm glad you asked," the Captain said with a grin. "Back when I was growing up, my father and most of the other fellas all had their own boats, but none of them ever called themselves captain. But when I took over my dad's boat, I made it point to let people know that I was the new captain."

Davidson was somewhat relieved that the Captain had some real experience on the water. The group sat silently for a few moments, enjoying the wind and sun.

"There's the old lighthouse," James pointed out.

"Do they still use that?" Mrs. Simpson asked.

"No, not anymore," the Captain answered. "It's still a good spot for fishing, though," he added, glancing at Davidson, "if you ever get your own boat."

"I doubt I'd have the time to use it," Davidson said.

Twenty minutes later, the lighthouse was out of sight. Everything seemed to be going very well when the boat suddenly lurched to a halt, making a deep grinding noise in the process. Everyone, including James, was thrown to the deck.

"Cut the engine, cut the engine," the Captain shouted. James pulled himself up and turned the key, but smoke was already leaking through the cracks around the trap door in the deck above the engine compartment.

"Hit the blower," the Captain ordered.

James flipped the blower switch to the "on" position as the Captain crawled over and opened the trap door, releasing a large cloud of oily smoke.

"What happened?" Davidson asked.

"The propeller must have hit something," the Captain said. "Sandbar or something, maybe."

"Why is it smoking like that?" Mrs. Simpson asked.

"Looks like the engine's locked up," the Captain replied. "The propeller must be jammed." He leaned over the stern, trying to see the propeller. "I can't see anything. James?"

James stood near the wheel while the Captain pushed himself up. "I'm really sorry, Mr. Peters…" he said.

"Hey, it wasn't your fault," the Captain reassured him. "I need you to turn that blower on and then get on the radio and call for a tow."

"I did turn the blower on," James replied.

The Captain tried the blower switch a few times but got no response. Then he tried the radio. "No electric. Pull up that battery hatch and take a look."

James complied. "There's water leaking in."

The Captain got down on all fours for a better look. "Whatever we hit must have knocked the whole thing loose. James, better drop anchor."

"So there's no radio?" Davidson asked, beginning to grow concerned.

"No power for the radio," the Captain responded. "I don't suppose you have a cellular phone?"

"I left it in the car," Davidson said.

"Here's a radio," Eileen said, holding up a portable AM/FM/Weather radio that had been tucked into the compartment beside her seat.

"Thanks, honey," the Captain said as he leaned over to take the radio from her, "but this radio doesn't transmit. We need one we can talk on."

"Look," Mrs. Simpson said, pointing to the gurgling water that was filling the battery and engine compartments.

"Man, I really screwed up," James said.

The Captain motioned James into the cockpit area and set the radio on the front seat. "Better break out the vests and the raft," he said quietly, even though they could all hear him.

James handed out the life vests first.

"The thick part of the vest should be toward the front, like this," the Captain demonstrated. "Eileen, your vest is a little different. Mrs. Simpson, you need to run that strap around her back. Eileen, honey, I'm going to tie this little whistle to your vest. If something happens and you fall into the water, you blow on that whistle and James will come get you."

James did not bother with the straps on his vest. Instead, he began to pull a rectangular case from the storage area in the forward hold. The water was now overflowing the compartments and spilling onto the deck.

"Go ahead and pull it," the Captain said in response to a questioning look from James.

James pulled the CO_2 release and the raft expanded, forcing the Captain and James to move out of its way.

"Okay, get it over the side and secure that line," the Captain ordered.

It was obvious to Davidson that the raft was not going to hold all of them. "Is there a paddle?" he asked.

"I'll check," James said, ducking his head into the forward hold. "I don't see a paddle. Just this pole."

"I gave the paddle to my daughter. She, uh…" the Captain trailed off. He looked down and ran his hand across his hair. "All right, this is what we'll do." He motioned for James and Davidson to come closer, and he whispered to them to prevent Mrs. Simpson and Eileen from hearing.

"No way," James protested upon hearing the Captain's plan.

"It's the only way," the Captain said.

"I'm the one who screwed up," James said.

The Captain glanced at Mrs. Simpson, who by now knew what the discussion was about, then looked back at James. "I'll be all right," he said. "Besides, they'll need someone young and strong to look after them."

"I think we're sinking," Eileen said calmly, noticing the water lapping over her feet.

"That's why were getting in the raft," Mrs. Simpson said.

"Mr. Davidson, you get in first while we hold the raft," the Captain said.

It was easier said than done, but Davidson got in and then helped Mrs. Simpson plop over. James then lowered Eileen into the raft, but paused before getting in himself.

"Go on," the Captain ordered.

"You should keep one of the flares," James said, handing the Captain a flare. "I'm sorry, Mr. Peters…"

"Now listen to me…listen," the Captain said, putting his hand on the teenager's shoulder to get him to look up. "You can't spend the rest of your life mopin' about every mistake you ever made. That's not why God put you here."

"Yeah, but this is…" James started.

"Just promise me you'll get over it," the Captain asked. "No matter what."

"I'll try," James said.

"Okay," the Captain said. "Go on, now."

James squeezed into the remaining space in the raft and Eileen noticed that the Captain was not coming. "Aren't you coming?" she asked the Captain as he untied the raft's line.

"No, honey," he told her. "I'm going to stay here and try to fix the radio. If I can get it fixed, I'll call the Coast Guard and tell them to come get you."

The raft was already drifting away in the current. "Okay," Eileen said, waving good-bye.

The others just looked on as the Captain waved back, each of them wondering if he would really be able to get the radio working.

* * * * *

After about two hours of mostly silence, Davidson saw something on the horizon.

"What's that?" he asked. "It looks like land."

"That must be the point," James said.

"So the current is taking us in," Mrs. Simpson said.

"No, I don't think so," James responded. "The point's a thin strip that sticks out pretty far."

"What lies beyond the point?" Davidson asked.

"Open sea," James said. "Nothing but ocean."

"Maybe we should try to paddle, then," Davidson suggested. James and Mrs. Simpson agreed, and for the next half hour they all leaned over the side and tried to paddle with their hands.

"I don't think we're getting any closer," Davidson finally said, exasperated. "We haven't done anything but rub our arms raw."

"It looks like we're closer," Mrs. Simpson said.

"We're closer to the point," James said, "but only because the current is taking us farther up the coast."

Dejected, they rested quietly. When the raft was almost parallel to the point, Davidson started eyeing the jutting shoreline. Then he pulled out his wallet and removed a twenty-dollar bill, sticking it in his breast pocket. "Mrs. Simpson, do you have a pen and paper?" he asked.

"Yes, I think so," Mrs. Simpson said, rummaging through her purse. "Here."

"Thanks," Davidson said. He jotted down a note and returned the pen. Then he pulled a plastic sandwich bag from his front pants pocket.

"I almost forgot I had this," he said, putting the note and the twenty into the crumb-laden bag and "zipping" it closed.

"I wouldn't worry about your money gettin' wet," James said wryly.

Davidson ignored the comment. "How far do you think we are from the point?" he asked.

"I don't know," James answered. "Couple of miles, at least."

"That's really our last chance," Davidson said, "and it'll be getting dark soon."

"What are you thinking?" Mrs. Simpson asked.

"When I was younger, I used to swim laps at the pool each summer," Davidson said. "I did about half a mile a day, three days a week. I used to be able to do a mile easy. Breast stroke, anyway."

"Swimming in the ocean isn't the same as a pool," James

cautioned.

"I know," Davidson said, taking off one of his shoes.

"Do you really think you could swim that far now?" Mrs. Simpson asked, her brow starting to wrinkle.

Davidson paused. He looked at the point again, then looked down and patted his lumpy belly. "Probably not," he sighed.

Mrs. Simpson sat back, relieved for the moment that she had talked some sense into the man. But Davidson then resumed what he had been doing, removing his other shoe and his life vest. "I thought you said you couldn't make it," she protested.

Davidson removed his belt and then looked at Mrs. Simpson. "Nevertheless," he said solemnly, and then slipped over the side into the water.

"Mr. Davidson!" James started to object, but backed down when he saw the look in Davidson's eyes.

"Don't forget about me if you get rescued first, okay?" Davidson said with a confident grin.

"Of course we won't forget," Mrs. Simpson said, not knowing what else to say.

Eileen, who had been mysteriously preoccupied with her doll for most of the time in the raft, had taken notice of Davidson's decision to swim for it. "Good-bye," she said.

"And good luck," James added.

The remaining raft members watched as Davidson slowly breaststroked his way toward the shore.

* * * * *

Davidson was scared. He had quickly discovered that James had been right—swimming in the open sea was not at all like swimming in a pool. He was smart enough to know that part of the fear stemmed purely from psychological factors. He knew, for example, that there were no sides to grab if he got tired, and no shallow end to stand up in if he swallowed water or needed to stop for some reason. The only way that he could rest was to turn over and do the elementary backstroke for a few minutes at a time.

He also knew that he faced very real physical challenges. Even though the water was fairly calm, he still had to time his strokes so that he could take his breaths between wave crests. The distance, also, was daunting, and it seemed at times that he was making no headway at all—at least, not toward the shore. The current, though, was moving him up the coastline, and he worried that he would be swept past the point.

He tried to swim freestyle, and he noticed that he made much better progress. It was so exhausting, however, that after no more than a minute or two he had to switch to elementary back stroke and ended up gasping for several minutes. It frightened him so much that he thought about returning to the raft. He looked back and could still see it, but it was much farther away than he had anticipated. He figured that he was either making more progress than he at first thought or the current was somehow pulling the raft away. As he switched back to breast stroke, and once again saw how distant the shore was, he felt a horrible sense of dread.

* * * * *

The sun had gone down and Mrs. Simpson was trying to get Eileen to go to sleep.

"But I'm hungry," Eileen said.

"Here," she said reaching into her purse. She pulled out a roll of breath mints and gave one to Eileen. "It's all I've got."

Eileen put the mint in her mouth and leaned against Mrs. Simpson.

"There's the moon," James said, nodding toward the shoreline.

"Well, at least Mr. Davidson will have some light to swim by," Mrs. Simpson said. "Do you think he'll make it?"

"I don't know," James answered.

* * * * *

Davidson was on the downside of what had been his second wind when he noticed clouds moving in from behind. The wind continued to pick up and soon the moon was just an obscure glow on the horizon. Then the wind became a squall and the rain made it hard for Davidson to see the lights on shore, but he knew he was close because he could hear the waves crashing. Eventually he was able to make out the dim silhouette of the rocks that were taking the beating.

Frightened, exhausted and nearing the turbulent beach, he summoned enough breath and enough courage for a simple prayer. "Not my will, Lord, but thine be done."

* * * * *

"That was some storm last night, huh?" Billy commented as he and his older brother, Thomas, scoured the beach.

"Maybe we'll find something," Thomas said. "Dad said that after that hurricane last year people found all kinds of stuff."

"What's that?" Billy asked, looking down the beach.

"C'mon," Thomas said, starting to jog toward the dark

mass. "Maybe it's a whale."

As the two boys approached, they realized that what they had found was not a whale. It was a man, lying face down, with one arm extended.

"Is he dead?" Billy asked, keeping his distance.

"I don't know. Hey, look!" Thomas noticed a plastic bag beneath the man's extended hand. "There's money in it," he whispered loudly.

Billy kept his distance. "Maybe we should tell somebody."

"Maybe he was a drug smuggler or something and got caught in the storm," Thomas speculated.

"I think we should tell Mom and Dad," Billy said.

"Okay, okay, but I wanna get the bag first."

Billy watched with nervous curiosity as Thomas cautiously approached the man. Thomas reached down, slowly at first, then snapped up the bag and ran back past Billy.

"Wait! Wait!" Billy yelled, trying to catch up as Thomas headed for the dunes.

* * * * *

In the opposite direction, farther down the beach, Susan Emerson was taking her morning jog. She worked mids as an RN at the hospital and liked to exercise after her shift. She was a little surprised when she saw the two boys because usually there were no people on the beach so early. As she watched the boys disappear over the dune, she noticed something in the corner of her eye.

She rushed over to the man after she saw him and instinctively thought to turn him over. For a split second she hesitated, wondering how decomposed the body might be, then she took a breath and rolled him onto his back. She spread his arms out and checked for a pulse. Then she pulled her cell phone from her fanny pack and made a call.

* * * * *

Thomas and Billy were catching their breath by the soda machine outside the Beach Road Grocery when Thomas opened the bag. "It's a twenty," he said. "And there's a note."

"What does it say?" Billy asked.

"Oh, man," Thomas said as he read it. "We better tell the cops."

The two boys got on their bikes and headed for the beach patrol station, which was only about half a mile away.

* * * * *

"Granny, are we going to die?" Eileen asked.

Mrs. Simpson opened her mouth to speak but could not.

"We all have to die sometime," James said, wondering to himself if Davidson and the Captain had made it through the storm.

"But now it's daytime, the storm is over and someone is bound to see us," Mrs. Simpson said as cheerfully as she could, hoping to counter the grim reality of James' statement.

"But now I'm *really* hungry," Eileen said. "And I've got a headache."

"Don't worry, honey," Mrs. Simpson tried to reassure the girl. "Your Mom and Dad must certainly be out looking for us."

"Yeah, but we didn't tell them we were going on a boat," Eileen reminded her grandmother.

Mrs. Simpson looked at James with concern.

* * * * *

"You boys did the right thing bringing this to me," the officer said. "We just got a 911 call about the man on the beach, but they didn't know about the note. Thanks."

"You're welcome," Thomas said.

"I called your folks," the officer said. "They want you to come back home."

"Okay," Thomas said. He and Billy started to leave, but Thomas stopped and turned back around. "Uh…Mr. Harris?"

"Yes?" the officer responded.

"This was in the bag, too," Thomas admitted, pulling the twenty out of his front shorts pocket.

Officer Harris took the bill and examined it. "I see. This could be important evidence." Then he kneeled down to look Thomas in the eye. "You're a good kid, Thomas. Stay that way, okay?"

"Okay," Thomas agreed, not quite sure what the officer meant.

* * * * *

The Coast Guard cutter got the call just after eight a.m. and changed course to head past the point. Two lookouts went forward with binoculars and started to scan the horizon.

"Nothing yet," the port lookout radioed to the bridge.

"Ya think they survived that squall last night?" the starboard lookout shouted to his counterpart.

"It was probably the squall that capsized them," the port

lookout said.

"Naw, it wasn't that bad," the starboard lookout commented. "Last night on the radio, though, I heard that a woman had called in saying her husband had taken some tourists out and never came back."

"I bet that's who we're looking for," the port lookout said. "Hey, looks like the sun's trying to come out."

The starboard lookout watched as the sun's rays began to pierce the overcast sky. He had always loved a changing sky, and his gaze followed the rays down to the water. "Like the finger of God…" he muttered to himself.

"What?" the other lookout asked.

"Nothing," he said. But where the sun's rays met the water, he saw something. "Wait a minute. I think I've got something off the starboard side."

"I've got it, too," the port lookout said, then remembered to use his radio. "Something off starboard."

"Good eyes, boys," came the radio reply from the bridge. "We'll tell the chopper."

A few moments later, a helicopter came up fast from behind the ship, catching the two lookouts by surprise as it passed low overhead.

"We must spend an awful lot of money on these searches," the port lookout said as the helicopter flew off into the distance.

"Yeah," the starboard lookout agreed, "but like the Good Book says, if you have a hundred sheep and just one gets lost, you'll still leave the other ninety-nine to go look for it."

"I wonder why?" the port lookout pondered.

Before long, the helicopter spotter was on radio. "Two adults and one child, confirmed. Proceed on present heading. We're going for the other guy."

The two lookouts glanced at each other and said in unison "What other guy?"

* * * * *

At the hospital, James and Mrs. Simpson were in the emergency room with Eileen's parents and James' mother. One of the doctors on duty had checked them out and they were now waiting on the other doctor to finish examining Eileen.

"The deputy said they were flying Captain Parker to shock-trauma," Mrs. Simpson was telling the others. "I guess it's because he was in the water all night."

As she was speaking, the doctor and a nurse came around the corner with Eileen between them.

"She'll be fine," the doctor said.

"I saw him," Eileen said. "I saw Mr. Davidson."

"You did?" Mrs. Simpson asked.

"Here in the hospital?" James asked.

"Who's Mr. Davidson?" Eileen's mother asked.

"He's the guy who swam to shore," James answered.

"Mr. Davidson has been admitted for overnight observation, but he seems to be all right," the nurse said.

"We passed him in the hallway," Eileen said. "He was in a wheelchair. He said he had to go."

"I think they were just taking him to his room," the doctor added.

"Did he say anything else?" James asked.

Eileen smiled. "He said he'd see us later."

THE END

THE

PAGEANT

"I don't know what you're planning to do, but you should sleep it off tonight before you go making hasty decisions," Mr. Sullivan advised.

"I know what I'm doing," Patrick said as he stuffed three small bottles of water into his knapsack.

"I know what he's up to," his girlfriend said as she walked into the kitchen and sat down at the table beside Mr. Sullivan. "He's off to kill the Queen."

"Patrick…" Mr. Sullivan started.

"Not quite, old man, but she's closer than she knows," Patrick said.

"The way things are going," the girlfriend added, "the royal family will put themselves out of business in a few years. Then you won't need to do anything." She tried to sound aloof, but she was really hoping to make him stop and think.

Patrick had just finished filling his bag and spun his head around with a glare. "I don't care about the royals one way or the other. They're just a symbol, and that makes them a target."

"What's this passion all about?" Mr. Sullivan asked. "Things are a lot different now. You've got nothing to complain about."

"You can't change my mind. I'm off," Patrick said. He hurried into the hallway, picked up his other bag, and was out the front door before the other two could think of anything else to say.

* * * * *

"Michael, you're the best looking angel I've ever seen," Mr. Perry said.

"Thanks, Dad," his seven-year-old replied.

"Are you sure you can't come?" Mrs. Perry asked her husband as she started to remove the costume from Michael. "You know who's supposed to be there."

"I don't really care about them, honey," her husband said. "It's you two I'll miss. But Mr. Coates was adamant, especially after last year's debacle. If I had known ahead of time…."

"I know," Mrs. Perry assured him.

"It's okay, Dad," Michael added.

"Ohhh, you're a good boy," Mr. Perry said, picking Michael up. "Now it's off to bed. You want to be well rested for tomorrow."

"But I'm not sleepy," Michael protested.

Mr. Perry glanced back at his wife and they both smiled

as she followed them to Michael's bedroom.

* * * * *

After driving most of the night, Patrick pulled off the road a few miles from his ultimate destination and walked the rest of the way through the woods. He stopped at the tree line to survey his objective. It was a large stone church. Anglican. Neo-Gothic. Enveloped that morning in a thick, wet mist. To Patrick, it seemed appropriately surrealistic.

After about fifteen minutes, seeing no sign of activity, Patrick dashed across the grassy yard to a side door. On previous scouting visits, he had noticed choir members, maintenance men and others using the door, so he assumed that it would be a good "back way" in. It was also the only door, except for the double doors in the front, that lacked a deadbolt. His bolt cutter made quick work of the padlock and he was in. He put the broken lock in his bag, pulled out an identical padlock, positioned it in the hasp, and closed the door behind him. He hoped that the first person to use the door would then assume that the door had been mistakenly left unlocked overnight, or opened by an early arrival. It was a risk, especially with the security that would be arriving later that day to prepare for the evening pageant, but he had no other choice.

Once inside, he headed up the back stairs to a storage room that he had noticed during a public tour he had taken on his last visit. (For an extra pound per person, his group had been given the deluxe tour, which included the upper portions of the church.) The small room had an opening that overlooked the pews from behind and provided unobstructed line-of-sight all the way to the altar, which had been temporarily turned into a stage for the pageant. He figured that the room had probably been used for lighting in the past, but had learned on the tour that all-new klieg lights had been installed the previous year with a new control room downstairs. Given the dust, he assumed that the storage room was now rarely used. Still, he was worried that someone might open the door and look in the room for some reason. As a precaution, he stacked some boxes in front of an old table that was against the wall, creating a hiding place beneath the table large enough for him to lie down and rest while remaining out of sight. He then set his watch alarm and, using his jacket for a pillow, laid down for a nap.

* * * * *

"Are you sure you don't have to go?" Mrs. Perry asked one more time.

"Mom, trust me," Michael said precociously.

"All right, then, let's go," she said.

They arrived at the church about an hour early, but there were already so many cars that they had to park on the grass.

"Why are there so many policemen?" Michael asked before they got out of the car.

"It must be extra security for the royal family," she said, setting the parking brake as she answered.

"Will the Queen be here?" he asked.

"No, honey, I don't think so," she said, "but then, they never did tell us which ones would be coming. You're not nervous, are you?"

"I don't think so," he answered.

"Well, don't be," his mother said. "They're just people like the rest of us."

Two elderly women sat behind a folding table near the front door.

"Good evening," one of them said, looking first at Mrs. Perry and then noticing Michael. "You must be one our performers."

"Yes," Mrs. Perry said. "The Angel Choir."

"You'll need to sign in, then," the other lady said, offering a pencil.

"We just want to make sure that we don't start without any of the *important* people," the first lady added with a smile as Mrs. Perry signed. "Go through the doors and to your right. You're a bit early, so you'll have to wait while the older children warm up."

"That's all right," Mrs. Perry replied.

"If you're lucky," the first lady said, almost whispering, "there might be a few folding chairs left in the staging area."

"Thanks," Mrs. Perry said.

Mother and son entered the main foyer holding hands. The foyer was really just a bulge in the middle of a long service hallway that ran the length of the church. Two inner doors, one propped open, led to the pews. A handwritten sign was posted on the closed door, with an arrow pointing in the direction of the staging area.

"It certainly is crowded," Mrs. Perry said as they made their way down the hall, dodging adults with wine glasses and children of various sizes.

Michael just nodded. He was looking for his friends from his Sunday school class. They were all supposed to be there.

"Here's one," Mrs. Perry said, grabbing a gray metal folding chair that was leaning against the wall. "Do you see any other chairs?"

"I don't need a chair," Michael said.

"It's going to be at least half an hour before you go on," she said. "Why don't you go look for one?"

"Okay."

Michael followed the hall farther down and saw two of his friends.

"Hey, Michael," one of them said. "John said there was a secret passageway that goes upstairs. Wanna go?"

"Yeah. But I need to ask my mom," he answered.

"Okay. It's down at the other end of the hall," the other one said. "We'll meet you there."

"That's okay, my mom's on the way," Michael said.

The three boys, all in white and Michael in wings, darted down the hall and stopped at Mrs. Perry.

"Mom, can I go play upstairs for a while?" Michael asked.

"I don't know…" Mrs. Perry said.

"It's okay, Mrs. Perry," the older boy said. "My mom said we could."

"All right, but don't stay too long," Mrs. Perry hesitantly agreed. "And don't mess up your wings."

The boys scampered off. The "secret" passageway turned out to be nothing more than a narrow winding staircase at the end of the hall, and no one seemed to mind that the boys were going upstairs, perhaps because of their choir outfits.

* * * * *

Patrick had slept until early afternoon, when some technicians arrived downstairs and started testing the sound system. The waiting would have been unbearable had he not discovered an old Gideon's New Testament in one of the zippered outer pockets of his knapsack. He had put it there years ago, back when he was in college. Some stranger had just walked up to him on campus one day and handed it to him. He ended up reading more of the Bible that afternoon than he had read since childhood, even though it was the King James version.

Now, with all of the people and the noise downstairs, he felt it was safe to move around a bit. He got up from beneath the table to stretch, and then pulled a water bottle and some crackers from his pack. The thought that it might be his last supper shot through his mind without warning, but he suppressed it. Then, for the first time that day, he heard someone coming upstairs. He grabbed his pack and scurried back to his hiding place, forgetting that he had left the New Testament on the table.

* * * * *

"There's not much up here," the youngest boy said.

"Yeah, it's kinda disappointing," the oldest one said. "I thought there'd be a balcony or something."

"Maybe that's it," Michael said, pointing to a door.

The three boys looked at each other, wondering for a moment if they should. Then the oldest shrugged his shoulders, silently suggesting "why not?" and they moved toward the door. The oldest opened it and went in.

"Augh, it's just a big closet," he said.

The younger one entered, but Michael snagged a wing trying to get in.

"Hold still," the younger one said, returning to unhook the wing from the protruding lock plate in the door frame.

"I'd better take them off," Michael said. "Where are your wings?"

"My mom has 'em," the older boy said. "Here, put them

on this table."

Michael laid the wings on the table and noticed a New Testament. It seemed to be the only thing in the room that was not covered in a thick layer of dust. But then, it *was* a church, he thought.

"It's too dirty in here," the youngest one said.

The other two agreed and they moved back into the hallway.

"There's nothing worse than a dirty angel," Michael said.

"Do you think there are real angels?" the youngest one asked.

"Sure. Michael's named after one of them," the oldest said. "There are three of them in the Bible."

"Only three?" Michael asked.

"Well, only three with names," the oldest replied. "Michael, Gabriel...."

"Who's the third?" the youngest asked.

"I can't remember," the oldest said.

Then they heard a noise that sounded like it came from inside the room.

"What was that?" Michael asked.

They stood very quietly, nervously hoping that they would not hear anything more. Then the loud speakers kicked in downstairs and they heard an announcer welcoming the guests.

"The pageant's starting," the oldest one said with relief.

"We should go back," the youngest said.

The other two nodded in agreement and they headed toward the spiral staircase. By the time they made it to Mrs. Perry, the first choir had started to sing, complete with orchestra.

"See ya, Michael," the oldest said, waving as he and the

other boy continued down the hall.

Michael's return wave was cut short by his mother's interruption.

"Michael, where are your wings?" Mrs. Perry asked.

"I…I left them upstairs," he said.

"Well you'd better go back and get them," she said with a mildly scolding tone in her voice.

"Yes, ma'am." Michael did not want to go back upstairs alone, but for some reason he did not think to ask his mother to accompany him. He made it to the spiral stairs without getting nervous because there were still people milling about in the lower hall and foyer. He grew more apprehensive as he climbed the stairs, but was relieved to see that the light in the upper hall was still on. He approached the door to the room cautiously, remembering the earlier noise.

* * * * *

Still lying beneath the table, Patrick lifted himself onto his elbows and shook his head in disbelief after he heard the boys go back downstairs. He commended himself for stacking the boxes around the table. Then he heard the music begin and he realized that it was time. Grabbing his bags, he got up from his hiding spot and put his things on top of the table.

He stuck his pistol in the waist of his pants, figuring that it might come in handy during his escape. Then he pulled his hunting rifle from its carrying bag. He put it on the table and pulled a box of ammunition from his knapsack. He tensed when he heard the noise behind him.

Michael pushed the door open slowly and stepped into the room. He gasped when he saw the man.

Patrick pulled the handgun from his waist and spun around in one quick motion. In a split second, Patrick had his adversary backed against the wall, contemplating the business end of a 9mm at nose length. Although he was trying desperately to be the cool assassin, Patrick was nervous and sweating, and it took him a moment to realize that his adversary was just a child.

"I just came to get my wings," Michael uttered.

Patrick took a deep breath, retracted his pistol a few inches, and motioned for the boy to move farther into the room. Michael, nearly as white as his costume and almost shaking, complied. Patrick put his left forefinger to his lips and Michael nodded in understanding. Then Patrick closed the door and Michael waited anxiously for his eyes to adjust to the dim light.

Patrick put the pistol on the table and began loading the rifle, glancing at Michael every few seconds from the corner of his eye. He noticed the wings on the table, partially covered by the rifle's carrying bag, but continued with his work.

With the rifle in his right hand, Patrick moved toward the back wall. He slid a piece of plywood aside with his left hand, revealing a hole in the wall. Instantly, the music and singing grew louder, rushing through the hole like water through a breached hull. Patrick took a prone position on the floor and started aiming through the hole, with Michael frozen a few feet to his right.

It was not long before Patrick had his target in his sights, but something was wrong. At first Patrick thought it was just a case of nerves, but then he realized that it was the boy. He could feel Michael staring at him. After a minute or so, Patrick was so irritated by it that he postponed his shot and rose up on his knees.

He was almost eye to eye with Michael and all of the horrible options were rolling through his mind faster than he could control them. First he thought that he would take one shot, hit or miss, and run. Or maybe allow for two shots, in case the first missed. But he had not planned on any witnesses, much less a child. Without a silencer, he could not shoot the boy without revealing himself. He could take one shot with the rifle, then shoot the boy with the pistol, then run.

No, no, no, he thought. He was not a child killer. He would take two shots at his target just as he had originally planned, and then run, leaving the boy in the room. Surely the boy would not be able to give an accurate description. But they had now been staring straight at each other for a good 30 seconds or so—plenty of time to remember a face.

They were both startled when Patrick's watch alarm went off. Patrick fumbled to shut it off, trying to cradle the rifle in one arm as he did so. He looked at Michael again, as if to ask why he was there and what he should do now. Then he glanced at the hole in the wall to see if it would remind him, but it did not.

With a heavy sigh, Patrick stood up and put his rifle back in its bag. Then he put the pistol in his knapsack which, in turn, he slung over his shoulder. He picked up the rifle bag but, noticing the wings, set it down on the floor. He handed the wings to Michael and paused a moment to look the boy in the eye. Then he picked up the rifle bag and turned toward the door to leave.

"Wait," Michael said, picking up the New Testament. "This is yours, isn't it?"

Patrick extended his free hand to accept it. "Yes. Thanks."

Patrick turned right when he left the room and Michael,

wings in hand, turned left. When Michael got to the top of the spiral stairs, he turned and looked to the far end of the hall just in time to see Patrick at the top of the other stairs, looking back at him. Then they went their separate ways.

* * * * *

"Where have you been?" Mrs. Perry asked as her son approached. "I was starting to get worried."

"Don't worry, Mom," Michael said. "I was just getting my wings."

THE END

THE PITCH

"Thank you, Ankles!" the members of the opposing team shouted in unison.

Timmy "Ankles" Anderson tucked the ball and glove under his arm and left the mound with his head hung low. The last miserable game of a long, miserable season was over.

"Fellas, I know you're disappointed," Timmy's coach said as the team gathered around the dugout, "but the season's over and now it's pizza time!"

"Yeah!" Timmy's teammates agreed.

Timmy was less enthusiastic. The other guys were too nice to say anything—the coach would not allow it, anyway—but Timmy knew they were all blaming him. The only game they had won that summer was the one that Timmy did not make because he had gone to the beach with his family.

"We'll get 'em next year, Tiger," the coach said, lightly jabbing Timmy's shoulder.

"You should've let Craig pitch," Timmy said. "We might have won."

As the other team members grabbed their gear and headed to the parking lot with their parents, the coach held Timmy back for a moment. "Hey, c'mon," he said. "Craig's a good kid, but we both know he only won that July 4th game because the other team couldn't hit."

"Yeah, but…" Timmy started.

"No buts. Tell me what you're gonna do about it," the coach said, repeating his conclusions from an earlier discussion on the same topic.

"Practice," Timmy answered.

"That's right," the coach said. "If you want to be good, you've got to work at it. All the daydreams and good intentions in the world won't amount to a hill o' beans without work."

Timmy had heard the speech before.

* * * * *

At home that evening, Timmy went into the kitchen to thank his Mom for coming to the game.

"You're welcome, sweetie," she said as she washed the dishes. "Your father got some good shots of you with the video camera."

"Great," Timmy said sarcastically.

"If you don't like it, you don't have to play," his Mom responded.

"But that's just it," Timmy explained. "I do like it. Why can't I be good at it?"

"You are good," his Mom said. "You made pitcher this year, didn't you?"

"Yeah, but only because everyone else…" he started.

"I told you not use that kind of language, young man," his mother rebuked him. "You're just feeling sorry for yourself."

Timmy's younger sister had been sitting at the table, observing intently. "Why did they call you Ankles?" she asked.

Her mother started to shake her head, but Annie was too young to know any better.

"Because I pitch too low," Timmy said.

"Is that bad?" Annie asked.

"Yes, because I end up walking a lot of guys," Timmy explained.

"What does that mean?" Annie asked.

"It means they get on base and the other team wins, and we lose," Timmy said.

"That *is* bad," Annie said as her mother successfully fought off a grin.

"It's just not fair," Timmy said.

"What's not fair?" his mother asked.

"Why would God make me love baseball so much, but not give me the talent to play?" he asked.

"Oh, Timmy…" his mother started.

"I know, I know," Timmy said. "The Lord works in mysterious ways."

"Just have faith, honey," his mother said, brushing her hand across his hair.

* * * * *

By Thanksgiving weekend, Timmy had almost forgotten the previous season and was looking forward to Christmas. At the discount mall with his family, he and his father split off from Annie and his mother to buy gifts.

"Dad, look," Timmy said, directing his father's attention to a vendor's temporary stand in the middle of the mall.

"Hmm," his father muttered, eyeing the vendor's display of baseball memorabilia. He understood Timmy's enthusiasm, but he was cautious because he had heard about counterfeit autographs and other unscrupulous practices.

"Looks like you got a real baseball fan there," the old man said as Timmy scouted out the goods.

"Yeah, I guess so," Timmy's father said.

"Mostly junk," Timmy said after circling the stand.

"Ah, well, uh..." Timmy's father started, not wanting to offend the old man but secretly proud of his son's assessment.

"Oh, I know," the man admitted. "I used to collect a little bit myself. I do have something that might interest you, though."

The old man left his stool for a moment to retrieve an item hidden in the center of the cart-like stand.

"What is it?" Timmy asked, moving in for a closer view.

"You ever heard of a guy named Ripkin?" the man said, handing a baseball to Timmy.

Timmy was impressed when he saw the signature, but his father was skeptical.

"Is that real?" Timmy's father asked.

"Yup," the man said.

Timmy and his father looked at each other, then Timmy pulled out his wallet. He handed his father a baseball card. "Check the signatures," he said.

"Looks real," his father said, handing the card back to Timmy. "How much?"

"I think we can work something out," the man said.

Timmy held onto the ball, examining it in detail, while his

father haggled.

"Okay," his father said.

"Really?" Timmy asked. "Um…is this gonna be part of Christmas?"

"No," his father decided. "Let's just call it a special one-timer."

"All right!" Timmy said as his father paid the man.

"You hold on to that now," the man said. "It'll be worth something someday."

"Oh, it's worth something right now," the father said, returning his billfold to his pants pocket. "Now, where were we supposed to meet your mother?"

"In the ladies' section of…" Timmy started.

"Oh, yeah, that's right," his father remembered, pausing for a moment. "It seems like those department stores are nothing *but* ladies' sections."

"No, they've got men's stuff," Timmy said, not catching his father's meaning.

"Tell you what," his father said as they walked. "You go meet your Mom while I bring the car around. I'll wait for you at the front entrance, okay?"

"Okay," Timmy agreed.

"The store's front entrance, not the mall's," his father clarified.

"Okay," Timmy said again.

When Timmy arrived at the department store, he did not see his Mom or Annie, so he went inside. He saw handbags and accessories on his left, and perfumes and toiletries on his right. A woman with a small bottle of something turned toward him with a peculiar smile, but he kept a manly distance and continued farther into the store. He stopped at a junction between two main aisles, about 60 feet from the escalators. If his mother was in the store, she would have to go past this point to get out, he thought. Unless she was on the *second* floor….

He decided to wait a few minutes before looking upstairs, because his mother specifically said the women's section. Then he heard a commotion and turned to see what it was about. A girl, younger than Timmy but little bit older than Annie, had fallen on the down escalator. A woman carrying a bunch of shopping bags—probably the girl's mother, Timmy thought—was trying to help the girl up.

"Honey, get up," the woman said.

The girl tried to get up, but before she could the draw-string of her coat's hood got caught as the steps receded into the floor at the bottom of the escalator. The girl let out a single scream as she and her coat were jerked downward.

"Susie!" the woman exclaimed, dropping all of her bags.

The girl's fall had happened so quickly that the people behind the woman ended up knocking the woman over the top of the little girl. For a very long split second, no one said or did anything. Then the woman, now on her hands and knees, turned around and tried in vain to pull the little girl free.

"Stop the escalator, stop the escalator," the woman shouted as she tugged ferociously on the girl's coat.

The escalator was not really moving, but it was jerking and grinding, all the while eating away at the girl's coat.

"Hit the emergency button," a man on the escalator said.

By this time, two of the perfume ladies and a male clerk had rushed over and were trying to help free the girl.

"Take the coat off," the clerk said.

"I can't get her out," the woman cried. "I think it's got her arm."

"Hit the emergency stop," the same man on the escalator

repeated.

The two perfume ladies searched for the emergency button while the clerk and the woman tried desperately to keep the girl's arm from going under.

Timmy was stunned. He just stood there, watching. Then he saw why no one could find the emergency stop button. They were all too tall. From his vantage point, however, he could see the red emergency knob clearly. It was on the underside of the "hump" on the sidewall of the escalator, near the spot where the moving hand rail disappears into the lower portion of the sidewall. The red push-knob was protected by a clear hinged cover, to prevent people from accidentally hitting it with a bag or baby stroller.

"Can't you stop it?" the woman asked, crying almost as much as the little girl.

"Is there a stop button on the top?" one of the perfume ladies shouted upward.

It had only been a few seconds, but already a crowd was beginning to form. Timmy, however, could still see the emergency button. Then he remembered the baseball and pulled it from his jacket pocket.

"Get out of the way," he said to the people who were starting to move between him and the escalator. Then, motioning with both arms, he repeated himself a little louder. "Get out of the way."

As the people stepped back, Timmy trotted forward a little and then paused. With his eye on the red knob, he took a slow breath, did his best pitcher's wind-up, and threw as hard as he could.

The clear plastic cover exploded into pieces as the ball smashed through it and depressed the red knob. The escalator stopped.

"Thank God," the woman said, too focused on her little girl to notice the way in which the escalator had been turned off.

The clerk had already pulled out his Swiss Army knife and now began to cut through the remaining part of the girl's coat. While he was busy cutting, a security guard arrived and told the woman that an ambulance was on its way.

"Timmy," his mother said, approaching from behind with Annie in tow. "I thought we were going to meet up front?"

"You said the ladies' section," Timmy said.

"Well, I meant ladies' clothes," she explained, "but that's okay. What's all the commotion about?"

"Some girl fell on the escalator," Timmy answered.

"I hope she's all right," his mother said, genuinely concerned.

"I think she'll be okay," Timmy said as the three of them started toward the front of the store.

"What?" his mother asked, suspicious of Timmy's half-cocked grin and aware that people were staring at them.

"Hey, Ankles!" a boy about Timmy's age shouted from the crowd.

The boy stepped forward and Timmy vaguely recognized him as a player from one of the other little league teams. The boy held up Timmy's ball, then tossed it. As Timmy two-handed the catch, the boy nodded in respect. Then the people who had witnessed Timmy's pitch began applauding. Timmy tipped his baseball cap in humble acknowledgment. Young Annie waved, assuming that all of the attention was just part of the normal shopping experience. Timmy's mother scrunched her face in bewilderment, looking first at the crowd and then at Timmy.

"All right, I give up," his mother said. "What's going on?"

"Well, I guess..." Timmy began, "I guess God isn't so mysterious after all."

THE END

THE
PILGRIMAGE

"That had to be the filthiest bathroom I've ever seen," Ellie Hargrave said as she took her seat on the bus.

"The men's room had two lines for two stalls," her husband Scott responded. "Unfortunately, I chose the short line and ended up with the stall that had no toilet."

"Nothing?" Ellie asked.

"Just a drain in the ground," he said. "I wouldn't have touched the other toilet, anyway. Some of the other guys said it was too dirty to use."

"You'd think the Egyptian tourism people would do something," Ellie said. "I mean, the main crossing over the Suez Canal and they only have one filthy bathroom for an entire convoy of buses. It's ridiculous."

"Well," Scott said, "I think there's another city farther north that's actually the main crossing. This must be the truck route or something."

"You were right about taking those pills this morning,"

Ellie added. "It's probably another six or seven hours 'til Israel, and Tamar said no more rest stops until the border."

Tamar, the young Egyptian tour guide on the Hargrave's bus, stood up in the front of the bus to make an announcement using a microphone and the bus' PA system. Another Egyptian, more serious looking, was in the seat behind the driver.

"Ladies and Gentleman," Tamar began. "Ah, as you know, we had to get this extra bus because we had a few more people than we expected. But, uh, you can enjoy it—you know, spread out if you like and use the extra seats. Now I would like to introduce Mohammed. He is going to ride with us across the desert. As I told you, the Sinai is, for us, the eastern desert, and the Sahara is the western desert. Mohammed, you notice, is carrying a rifle. There is no need to worry though, it is just a precaution. He is a policeman. There will be a policeman on every bus. It is standard procedure. How do you say it in America? No big deal, yes? You with me? Okay, good."

Tamar stooped to speak with the driver for a moment, being careful to cover the microphone so no one else would hear.

"Uh, our driver has just told me that we will have to wait for the next ferry," Tamar continued. "As I said, we normally do not have this many buses, so we did not fit. When the ferry comes back across, it will unload, and then we will be first."

"Tamar," Ellie asked, raising her hand, "how long will that take?"

"I do not know exactly how long it will be," Tamar answered. "It should not be too long. It only takes, maybe, 20 minutes for the ferry to go and unload."

"Are the other buses going to wait?" a man in the back asked.

Tamar consulted with the driver, who spoke in muffled Arabic over the radio for a minute or so. Then Tamar answered. "Ah, no. We, ah, we are, I mean, we would normally have to go in the convoy, but they do not want to hold the convoy up so…."

Tamar again consulted the driver. "The driver said that we will catch up. We will take, uh, a shortcut. You know what I mean when I say shortcut? Okay, good. We will take a shortcut once we get to the other side of the canal."

Tamar sat down, out of view, in the front seat beside Mohammed. The Hargraves rolled their eyes at each other.

"At least we have air conditioning," Scott said. "Hey, do you want me to move across the aisle? You'd have more room."

Ellie smiled at her husband's consideration, still going strong after ten years of marriage. "No, but if you want to go ahead."

Scott eyed the two empty seats, but decided to stay put.

* * * * *

After almost an hour, the bus started to move. "Okay everybody," Tamar announced into the mike without getting up. "We will be first on the ferry and that means first off on the other side. We are going to stay on the bus to save some time, but I know you will want to get your cameras ready. As you know, when you cross the canal, you are going from one continent to another. We will be going from Africa into Asia. We will still be in Egypt, but the continent will be Asia."

As they began to cross the canal, Scott readied his video camera. The driver opened the back exit doors, which were just behind the Hargraves' seats, allowing the few people on the bus to get clear camera views rather than shoot through the windows. Intellectually, Scott understood the significance of crossing to another continent, but it felt less momentous than he had hoped.

"Is something wrong?" Ellie asked when he sat back down.

"I don't know," he said. "Egypt was sort of disappointing. I know I'm the one who wanted to see the Pyramids and all but...I guess my expectations were too high or something."

"They *are* just empty tombs," Ellie said. "But if I know you, I'd bet you were hoping for some sort of adventure, just like in the movies."

"Well..." Scott started with a small grin.

"Don't feel too bad," she said, putting her hand on his forearm and leaning toward him. "You might be surprised by the Holy Land tour. Galilee is beautiful, and Jerusalem is really fascinating. Trust me, you'll like it."

"I hope so," Scott said. "Maybe the tour group will have some interesting people."

"That's the spirit," Ellie said, returning to her paperback.

After unloading from the ferry, the bus followed some trucks along the main highway for a short while, but then pulled onto a narrower road. There was a long fence with barbed wire stretching along one side of the road, and sand dunes on the other.

Tamar stood up with the microphone. "This is the shortcut I told you about. On your left you see the fence. It is a military base over there, I believe. And on the other side you see the desert. Not much to see, really, but when we catch up to the convoy we will be closer to the Mediterranean. The Mediterranean Sea, you know? Okay, good. There will be more towns and things up there, but right now we are just going to do this shortcut for a little while longer to save time. Who knows, we might even beat the other buses."

Eventually the fence disappeared and there was nothing but sand and a few rocks in either direction. Scott had just reclined his seat, trying to get more comfortable, when a tremendous explosion threw him into the aisle and filled the bus with thick smoke. The bus careened off the road and rolled to stop in the sand, but did not tip over. Except for some coughing, it was eerily quiet.

"Ellie?" Scott called out as he got to his feet.

"I'm here," came a voice from the smoke. "I'm here. You okay?"

"Yeah," he answered. "You okay?"

"I think so," she said. "What happened?"

"I don't know," he said as he stood up, barely able to make out her figure through the smoke. "Grab the stuff."

An older man was struggling to push open the rear door when a teenaged boy came from the back of the bus to help. The boy got the doors open and hopped outside.

"Everybody out," the older man half yelled, holding the doors open and waving to Scott and Ellie to go past him. "Out the back, let's go!"

Scott and Ellie got off, followed by an older woman with a little girl of about six. The older man paused a moment, expecting more, but no one appeared.

"Come on," Scott said. "You've done all you can."

The older man peered one more time into the smoke, which was still pouring from the front of the bus, and then stepped off. "Move back, move back," he told the group, motioning with both arms.

They all stood in shocked silence, staring at the bus, except for the teenaged boy. He walked in a wide semicircle about 20 yards out from the wreckage, moving to get a better look at the damage to what used to be the driver's area. Scott noticed the lanky teen and followed.

"Unbelievable," the teenaged boy muttered as he viewed the front of the bus head-on.

"What in the world happened?" Ellie asked as she and the others approached Scott and the teenaged boy.

"It must have been a bomb," the teenaged boy said.

"A land mine, I guess," Scott added.

The old man had stayed back a bit, still viewing the bus from the side, but he could hear the others. "It must have been a land mine," he said. "Look at the hole it made."

The others followed him to the back of bus. There was a crater in the sand on the edge of the road a few yards behind the wreckage.

"Maybe terrorists did it," the teenaged boy speculated.

"Terrorists?" the older woman asked nervously.

"I'm not so sure it was terrorism," Scott said. "Remember those signs we saw this morning warning foreigners to stay on the main road? I thought Tamar said they were put up because there are still land mines in certain areas left over from the '73 war."

"I couldn't understand half of what he was saying with that microphone," the older man said. "I guess they could still have land mines that old."

"I know that in Israel they still have fields marked off because of land mines from the '67 war," Ellie said. "It's too expensive or maybe too risky to dig them up."

"From the looks of the damage," Scott added, "I'd say this

was probably some sort of anti-tank mine."

There was a lull in the conversation. Then, with the smoke clearing, Scott hopped back onto the bus through the back doors. He returned shortly.

"Anyone alive?" the older man asked.

Scott shook his head, looked down a bit, then looked at Ellie.

"Now what?" the teenaged boy asked.

"Maybe we should bury the dead," the older man said.

"I don't think we should," Ellie said. "I'm sure the police will want to see everything the way it is."

"Uh," Scott cleared his throat. "My name is Scott Hargrave and this is my wife, Ellie. We were traveling by ourselves. I was just wondering if, uh, if any of you had any friends or relatives…still on the bus."

Scott was relieved when they all shook their heads, especially the little girl and the teenaged boy.

"I'm Howard Stoner," the older man said, extending his hand to Scott.

"My name is Molly," the little girl said as the two men shook hands.

"I'm her grandmother, Patricia Finley. But you can call me Pat."

"What happened to the bus?" little Molly asked.

"Shh," Mrs. Finley hushed her granddaughter and then looked at the teenaged boy.

"I'm Tom," the teenaged boy said.

No one pressed him for a last name.

"Let's see if we can pull the luggage out of the bottom," Scott suggested. "I know I've got some bottled water in my suitcase, if it didn't get blown up."

"I'll give you a hand," Stoner said.

The two men went over to the luggage compartment doors on the lower side of the bus, followed by the others. One of the doors had come loose in the explosion.

"Looks like we lucked out," Scott said when he saw the open compartment. He began to pull the suitcases out and hand them to Stoner who, in turn, lined them up in the middle of the road.

"Ellie, honey," Scott said, "why don't you and Mrs. Finley start going through the bags. Look for any kind of water, food, sunscreen, um, hats...anything that might come in handy. Start with ours."

"Okay," Ellie complied.

"This one's locked," Mrs. Finley noted.

"Let me see if I can pop it," Scott said, pulling out his Swiss Army knife. He struggled with it but was not able to get it open.

"Look," Ellie said, holding up a cellular telephone she had pulled from one of the bags.

"Try it," Stoner said.

Ellie began to dial but noticed the look of consternation on her husband's face.

"It's not going to work," Scott said. "There aren't any cell towers out here."

"Maybe it's a satellite phone," Tom said.

"No, I don't think so," Scott said.

"Nothing," Ellie said.

"What about the bus driver's radio?" Tom suggested.

"Good idea," Stoner said. The two of them went to check it out while Scott and Ellie stayed with the Finleys. Stoner quickly returned, visibly shaken.

"I've never seen anything like that," Stoner said.

Mrs. Finley took him by the arm and put one hand on his

shoulder to comfort him.

"What about the radio?" Scott asked.

"I don't know," Stoner said. "I didn't see it."

"It's shot," Tom shouted, hopping down from the front steps of the bus. "Blown to bits. Just like the driver. Tamar seemed to be in one piece, though."

Scott sighed and then said to Ellie under his breath, "I think *someone's* been playing too many video games."

"He's probably in shock, honey," Ellie said. "I bet we all are."

* * * * *

"I don't think anyone's ever going to come," Molly commented.

Several hours had passed since the explosion. They were now just sitting in the road hoping that eventually someone would drive by. The group had sorted through the luggage and put on lots of sunscreen lotion.

Scott and Tom had gotten their baseball caps from their bags. Tom had put a white hand towel beneath his cap, allowing most of it to drape over the back of his neck.

"I think the little girl's right," Stoner said. "We should start walking back."

"But shouldn't they be looking for us by now?" Ellie asked.

"Maybe the driver didn't tell anyone about the shortcut," Scott said. "What do you think, *Beau Geste*?"

"I bet he wasn't supposed to take the shortcut," Tom answered, apparently oblivious to his Foreign Legion fashion statement. "I bet they didn't tell anybody because they weren't supposed to go this way. There hasn't been any traffic on this road all day, except for us."

"That's what I was thinking," Scott said. "Does anyone remember how long we were on this road before the explosion? It was about an hour, wasn't it?"

"At least two hours, I think," Mrs. Finley said.

"I think she's right," Ellie said. "It was more like two hours."

"Well, that means we should be closer to the Mediterranean road than the Suez road, right?" Scott asked.

"What are you suggesting?" Stoner asked.

"I'm suggesting that we go forward, not back," Scott said.

"It couldn't have been two hours," Stoner said. "That would put us a hundred miles east of the Suez."

"Even if it's only fifty miles to the canal, it would still take at least two days for us to walk back," Scott argued. "And we know for sure that there's nothing back that way except a fence. No towns, no water, nothing. I think if we walk north, we'll hit the Mediterranean road in a few hours. Certainly no more than a day."

"But this road goes east-west, doesn't it?" Mrs. Finley asked. "Besides, what if the Mediterranean road is deserted just like this one?"

"It's not," Ellie assured her. "That's the main road between Cairo and Israel. There are several towns along it. There's bound to be traffic on it. I was on it the last time I was over here."

"If we're going to go, we should probably walk at night, when it's cool," Scott suggested.

"I think we should wait a little longer," Mrs. Finley responded. "Molly and I have been up since dawn, anyway. We can't stay up all night walking across the desert."

"I'm tired, too," Ellie said.

"Okay, okay," Scott said. "How about this: we'll sleep here for now. If anyone is looking for us, that will give them several more hours to find us. But just in case, I'll set my watch alarm for 4 A.M. That way, if no one comes tonight, we can get started tomorrow before the sun comes up. Agreed?"

"I guess that sounds reasonable," Stoner said.

"What about supper?" Molly asked.

"We have two packs of peanut butter crackers," Ellie said. "We also have two half-liters of water, plus the rest of the big bottle."

"A cracker each, then, and a swig or two from the bottle?" Stoner suggested.

"Yeah," Scott agreed. "We can eat the other pack for breakfast, if we need it. Better save the two small bottles for as long as we can, though, just in case."

Ellie handed out the crackers and passed the one-and-a-half-liter bottle around. When Scott got the bottle, he put the cracker to his lips but only pretended to eat it. He slipped it into his breast pocket when no one was looking. Then he took a long drink and passed the bottle to Stoner.

"This is all we're going to eat?" Molly said, holding up her cracker.

"This is an emergency," Mrs. Finley said. "We'll get some more tomorrow."

Stoner retrieved his garment bag from the luggage pile and spread it on the ground beside Molly. "You can sleep on this tonight. It should keep the sand off you."

"What do you say?" Mrs. Finley prompted.

"Thank you," Molly said.

"You're welcome," Stoner replied.

The rest of them pulled out various clothes from the luggage and used them in lieu of blankets and pillows.

* * * * *

The beeping of Scott's watch alarm was met with stiff resistance. Only Molly had gotten a decent night's rest. The others were less enthusiastic about getting up, especially because it had taken them so long to get to sleep in the first place.

"I guess this means no one's coming to the rescue," Ellie said, checking her own watch to make sure it was really 4 A.M.

"I've gotta take a leak," Tom said, getting to his feet.

"Does anyone have any tissues?" Scott asked.

Both Ellie and Mrs. Finley replied in the affirmative.

"So do you," Ellie added.

"Oh, that's right," Scott remembered, checking his pants pocket. "I almost forgot about the Egyptian toilet paper shortage."

"It seems especially acute at tourist sites," Stoner joked.

They had all been forewarned by their tour agents that public restrooms in Egypt were not adequately stocked. The locals seemed to appear out of nowhere whenever tourists found a bathroom, scalping sheets of T.P. like they were tickets to the Super Bowl. As a precaution, everyone in the stranded group had brought their own supply of travel tissues—even Molly.

"I've got mine," she said proudly, holding up her pack of tissues while everyone else smiled.

"Why don't you girls go around to the other side of the bus?" Scott said. "We'll go a couple of dunes over."

"I'd rather not go near the bus," Mrs. Finley said.

"Okay," Scott said. "Everyone spread out, find your own dune. I'm going on the other side of the bus."

"By the way," Ellie said to the group, "I highly recommend that you wear two pairs of socks today. It should help prevent blisters."

After regrouping, they agreed to put off breakfast until the sun came up.

"Honey, do you have your little flashlight?" Scott asked as he tried to read his small compass.

"Here," Ellie said, shining the light downward.

"All right," Scott said, pointing, "looks like north is that way. Everybody ready? We got the water?"

Ellie nodded and turned slightly to show her backpack, slung over one shoulder, in which she had packed the water and other supplies.

"Crackers?" Scott asked.

"Yup," Ellie replied.

"Sunscreen?" Scott continued.

"Check," Ellie said.

Scott paused a moment to think and then grinned a little. "T.P.?"

"Yes," the others replied in unison.

"Then let's go."

Scott and Tom led the way, with Ellie close behind. It soon became clear, though, that Stoner, Mrs. Finley and Molly required a slower pace.

"This sand is tough to walk in," Stoner said, noticing that Tom and the Hargraves kept stopping every now and then to let him and the Finleys catch up.

"Don't worry," Scott reassured him. "We're in no rush. We can stop every hour if we need to."

"Maybe every half hour," Ellie suggested out of concern.

"It's been almost a half hour now," Scott said. "Do ya'll want to take a break?"

"Please," Mrs. Finley said.

Mrs. Finley, a bit plump even for her age, plopped down on the sand and Molly joined her. The rest remained standing. Ellie let her backpack slide to the ground.

"Don't lose that," Scott warned.

"No way," Ellie said.

Scott looked back. He thought he could just make out the outline of the bus, but it was still dark and he could not be sure. He had hoped on doing about three miles an hour, but it was clear to him now that that was an unreasonable expectation. But even at two miles an hour, he thought, they would still cover 20 miles by the end of the day.

"That's five," Scott said, checking his watch. "Time to get going."

Stoner gave Mrs. Finley a hand up and the trek resumed. They continued for about 45 minutes and stopped again when the sun was just about to breach the horizon.

"I think we've got enough light for breakfast," Ellie said, pulling the last pack of peanut butter crackers from her backpack.

"I was hoping you'd say that," Tom said.

"Only one swig from the bottle, now," Scott said as Ellie opened one of the two half liters and passed it around.

Once again, Scott only pretended to eat his cracker, slipping it into his shirt pocket with the other one. He drank some water and then moved away from the group, looking out across the desert.

"We've got a long way to go on one cracker," Tom said quietly as he approached Scott from behind.

"I know," Scott said soberly, staring at the sandy desolation.

* * * * *

By midday it was sweltering. They were walking almost single file now. Scott took turns with Tom leading the way, checking his compass every few minutes to make sure they were still going north. Neither Stoner nor Mrs. Finley would go more than 20 or 25 minutes without asking for a break. Scott felt sorry for them, but he was sure that it would not be long before they reached the Mediterranean road.

He was sure, that is, until he saw a rocky hill up ahead. Then he began to worry. What at first appeared to be a large dune turned out to be a miniature mountain. It was only one hill, he thought, but the mountains were supposed to be to the south. He had expected the terrain to get flatter and flatter as they moved north. The unexpected hill made him wonder if he had made a mistake, if his compass was not working right. He grew anxious with the thought that he had taken the group south instead of north, away from help instead of toward it. He looked up at the sky.

"Tom," Scott called out. "Come here. Do you remember where the sun rose this morning?"

"Uh, no," Tom answered. "I wasn't really paying attention."

"Me neither," Scott sighed, stroking his chin.

"What's wrong?" Tom asked.

"Nothing, I hope," Scott said. "Listen, don't tell the others, but we need to make sure we're really going north. I don't know if the compass is working right."

"We'll know when the sun starts to go down," Tom said.

"We can't afford to wait that long," Scott said.

Ellie, too far away to hear the conversation, wondered what was going on. "Honey, isn't it about time for a break?" she asked.

"Yes, but let's stop over by those rocks," Scott said loudly enough for all to hear. "I want to climb up and see if I can spot a road or something."

They trudged through the sand for another 15 minutes before reaching the rocky hill. There was a large enough outcropping near the base to provide a little shade.

"Shade!" Ellie exclaimed as she entered the shadow of the rock. "I never thought I'd care so much about shade."

Mrs. Finley and Molly and Stoner all sat down around Ellie. Scott and Tom squeezed into the shadow, too. Scott remained standing, but Tom had to squat to get his face out of the sunlight.

"How about some water, honey," Scott asked his wife.

"We'll have to open the last bottle," she said.

"Well, this is a good place to do it," Scott said, sitting down Indian-style.

Scott took a drink and passed the bottle. "No sense in waiting, I guess," he told the others as he got back to his feet.

"Do you think it's such a good idea to go climbing?" Ellie asked.

Scott eyed the slope. "It is steeper than I thought," he admitted, "but I have to. What if there's a town or something just over one of the dunes? We don't want to walk the wrong way and miss it."

Tom stood up and for a moment Scott was afraid that he would mention the north versus south concern.

"I'll go with you," Tom offered.

"Fair enough," Scott agreed. "If I slip, you can catch me, okay?"

"You got it, Mr. H," Tom said.

Suddenly it was "Mr. H," Scott thought. Ellie picked up on it, too.

Scott looked for a good route and then started up, with

Tom close behind. The higher they climbed the more strenuous it became and soon Scott was wheezing. Under different circumstances, Scott probably could have tackled the climb with little difficulty. The lack of food, however, combined with the sun, the heat, the limited sleep, the seven-hour desert march, and sheer worry, seemed to be exacting their toll all at once.

"You okay?" Tom asked when Scott stopped just shy of the top.

"We're almost there," Scott said, wiping his brow with the back of his forearm, "but I've gotta stop for a bit."

Tom waited for a few moments, alternating his gaze between Scott and the small ridge just beneath the summit. "It's not much farther," he said.

Scott looked at Tom and then at the ridge. He could tell that Tom was eager to go on. "All right," he said, motioning with his head toward the ridge. "Go for it. Just be careful."

Tom climbed past Scott with relative ease, but had trouble getting over the final crest. He struggled to pull himself up, a foot slipping occasionally. After he finally pulled himself over the edge, he found that the other side was a fairly smooth rock face with a more gradual slope, giving him plenty of room to stand up.

Scott, breathing better now, looked up and saw Tom stand to his feet. "Can you see anything?" he asked. "Do you see any mountains?"

Tom stood for a moment with his hands on his hips. Gazing toward the horizon, he allowed the breeze coming over the rock face to cool him off. Then he looked back over his shoulder toward Scott. "No mountains," he replied. "It's all flat. You can see for miles."

Scott closed his eyes and leaned back against the side of

the rock. "Thank you, God," he thought.

"Hey," Tom shouted. "There's a town."

Scott perked up. "Are you sure?" he asked.

"I can see buildings," Tom answered.

"Only one town?" Scott asked.

"Yeah, just one," Tom said. "At least from what I can see."

"Where is it?" Scott asked. "What direction?"

"Looks like it's right where we were headed," Tom answered. "Guess you were right all along, Mr. Hargrave."

"Is there a road?" Scott asked.

"I don't know," Tom said. "I don't see one."

* * * * *

Scott and Tom returned to the base of the hill. After seeing Tom struggle, Scott had decided not to attempt the summit.

"Well?" Ellie asked.

"I saw a town or something," Tom said. "Definitely buildings. I think if we just keep walking the way we were going, we should get there pretty soon."

The others looked to Scott for confirmation.

"I must say, I'm glad Tom climbed up with me," Scott began. "I didn't make it all the way to the top. Good job, Tom."

Ellie eyed Scott with suspicious concern. "I guess it's not bad for someone pushing forty."

"Hey, hey, hey," Scott retorted. "Thirty-six is not the same as pushing forty."

"In this heat," Mrs. Finley said, "I'm surprised anyone could do it."

"Before we go," Scott said, "I need to find a little boy's

dune."

"Go right ahead," Stoner said. "I'm in no hurry to leave this shade."

Scott walked around the hill, out of sight of the others. He had a headache and felt dizzy. He removed one of the crackers from his shirt pocket and ate it. When he returned to the group, he saw Tom drinking.

"I don't want to drink it all up," Scott said, "but I sure could use a sip." Tom handed him the bottle. "Honey, do you have any aspirin?"

Ellie searched her backpack and pulled out her pill box, handing two tablets to her husband. "Headache?" she asked.

"Big time," Scott replied before swallowing the two pills. "Well, we've still got a little water left."

After Ellie re-packed the bottle, the group set off, with Tom in the lead. They had trudged for an hour or so when Molly ran up alongside of Scott.

"When are going to stop for lunch?" she asked.

Scott looked down at her for a moment. "Come here," he said, picking her up. "I know you're hungry. I'm hungry, too. But it shouldn't be long now before we come to a town and we can get something to eat."

"How long?" Molly asked.

"I don't know," Scott said. "I do have something that might help, but you have to promise to keep it a secret."

"I promise," Molly said.

Scott glanced about to make sure no one else was close enough to see, even though he knew that Ellie and Mrs. Finley, both behind him, were watching. He carefully removed the cracker from his shirt pocket.

"I found this extra cracker," he whispered. "You can have it, but don't tell anyone else about it, okay?"

"Why not?" Molly whispered back.

"They might feel bad because I gave the cracker to you and not to them," Scott said.

"Okay," Molly agreed, taking the cracker.

"What do you suppose those two are up to?" Mrs. Finley asked Ellie.

Ellie just smiled. Her eyesight was better than Mrs. Finley's and she had felt a twinge of spousal pride upon witnessing the cracker transaction.

After she had finished her snack, Scott put Molly down and she waited in place for Ellie and Mrs. Finley to catch up.

"Did you have an interesting conversation with Mr. Hargrave?" Mrs. Finley asked.

"Yes," Molly said, keeping her promise.

Before either of the two women could inquire further, Tom saw some buildings as he went over a small dune.

"There it is," Tom said.

"Finally," Ellie said as she and the others walked up the dune that had been blocking their view.

In eager anticipation, they picked up their pace.

"Something's wrong," Scott said as they neared the buildings.

"I don't see any people," Ellie noted.

"Me neither," Tom said.

"These buildings don't look finished," Stoner said as the group walked down an unpaved street in what appeared to be a small ghost town.

"They're just concrete shells," Scott said.

They walked for a few minutes past several unfinished buildings. On the other side of "town" they saw a paved road leading into the desert.

"No people, no cars," Tom said. "What is this place?"

"I think I know," Ellie said. "The last time I was over here, I remember the tour guide saying something about the population—something like, 95 percent of Egypt's population lives in the Nile delta, or along the Nile, or something like that. He said the government was trying to encourage people to move by building new towns or something."

"Why would anyone want to live here?" Tom asked.

"I'm not sure, but I think the government would build apartments and then let people live in them for free, or almost for free," Ellie said.

"I don't believe this," Scott said, his frustration showing.

"So there's no water?" Mrs. Finley asked.

"Do you see any water?" Scott shot back.

"Scott..." Ellie said, trying to calm him down.

"Let's follow the road," Tom said.

"Young man," Stoner started, "I don't think you understand. I'm not as young as you are. I can't just go, go, go, anymore. I have to rest."

"Okay, okay, look," Scott said. "Tom and Ellie and I will follow the road. Ya'll just wait here for a while."

Stoner and the Finleys found a spot in the shadow cast by the building closest to the road. The other three hit the pavement. They had gone about a mile or so when the road disappeared into the desert, covered by drifting sand. There were no telephone poles nor any other signs of civilization save the road and the buildings behind them. Scott sat down and put his head in his hands. Ellie and Tom joined him.

"We've had it," Scott said.

"Don't say that," Ellie said.

"I don't know, Mrs. Hargrave," Tom said, removing his hat and wiping his head with the towel. "He might be right."

"You didn't see anything else from the hill?" Scott

asked Tom.

"No," Tom answered.

"Then the best we can do is walk where we think the road should be," Scott said. "It appears to go north or northwest. Maybe we'll hit the main road."

"We're bound to hit the main road sooner or later," Ellie said, trying to be optimistic.

"Yeah, but 'later' might be too late," Scott said. "Just getting to the road doesn't mean there'll be water or food."

"What else can we do?" Ellie asked. "Let's go back and get the others."

Scott nodded and they walked back to the buildings. There they found Mrs. Finley holding Molly like a baby, although Molly was clearly too big for that.

"She was crying up a storm for a while," Stoner said. "Poor little thing."

"I don't blame her," Scott said.

"How much farther is it?" Mrs. Finley asked, assuming that the road from the buildings connected to the Mediterranean road.

"The road ends about 20 minutes from here," Tom said. "It's covered by sand."

Ellie saw the concern in Mrs. Finley's face and tried to preempt a break down. "It can't be far to the main road," Ellie said. "We'll just keep going in the direction the road was going."

"I feel too weak," Stoner said.

"Maybe we should sleep here," Ellie suggested. "We can get up tonight and walk when it's cool."

"You wanna sleep now?" Tom asked. "Won't that just put us a few hours closer to starvation?"

"Starvation's not the problem," Stoner said. "We could

probably go a couple of weeks or more without food. It's the water that's important. I doubt I'll last more than a day or two without water. I think the longest a person can go without water is about four days, but I don't know if that includes hiking across the desert."

"So we'll be a few hours closer to dying of thirst," Tom retorted. "What's the difference?"

"Tom, we've got to rest," Scott said. "I know you're young, but we've got to rest. Ellie's right. It will be better to walk at night. We'll lose less water that way."

"I've got an idea," Ellie said, rummaging through her backpack. "I don't know about the rest of you, but I've got a terrible headache, and I think I've still got some aspirin left in here somewhere."

"I don't know if I can handle aspirin on an empty stomach," Mrs. Finley said. "I'd hate to get sick now."

"She's right," Scott said.

"Here it is," Ellie said as she pulled out her pill box. "I was wrong. It's acetaminophen, not aspirin."

"It's a good idea, honey, but we don't have enough water," Scott said, holding up the half liter bottle, which was less than a quarter full.

"Hold on," Tom said, reaching behind his back with both hands. He pulled a can of soda from a fanny pack that had remained hidden beneath his untucked shirt. "I was saving this in case we got desperate."

"I think we're sufficiently desperate," Mrs. Finley said.

"Molly, have you learned to swallow pills yet?" Ellie asked.

"No," Molly said.

"I have some medicine that will make you feel better, but you have to swallow it," Ellie said, holding up one of the tablets and the bottle of water.

"I don't like medicine," Molly said, shaking her head and pulling back as Ellie drew closer.

"Ellie, honey," Scott said, "don't force it. We can't afford to have her start choking."

"All right," Ellie reluctantly agreed.

"Let Molly have the rest of the water," Tom said. "You guys can swallow the pills with my soda. It's pretty warm, though."

Molly cautiously accepted the water from Ellie. Then Ellie handed out the pills and Tom passed the soda around.

"I never thought I'd enjoy warm soda," Scott said.

"I never thought I'd like this fanny pack that my mom gave me," Tom replied.

"Where are your parents, if you don't mind my asking?" Scott asked, taking advantage of the opportunity.

"They're back home," Tom said. "They think I'm touring Israel with our church group. It's sort of a graduation present that some of the parents worked out with the church for the seniors, but anyone could sign up."

"So they don't know you're in Egypt?" Ellie asked.

"Nope," Tom said. "I was supposed to spend two weeks in Israel, but after the first week I told my friends I just had to see the Pyramids. They were too scared to leave the group, so I came by myself. I couldn't afford to fly, so I took the bus. I figured I would only spend three days here—one day down, one for the Pyramids, and one day back. That would still leave three more days in Israel before the flight back."

"I hope your parents bought trip insurance," Scott joked.

"In case I miss my flight?" Tom asked.

"Gentlemen, please, we should be trying to sleep," Stoner reminded them.

They all fell asleep much faster than the previous day, even though it was not yet dark. When Scott awoke, the stars were out and the others were still sleeping. He got up as quietly as he could, but Molly woke up. She motioned with her finger for him to come near.

"Did you find any more extra crackers?" she whispered.

Scott's heart sank. "No, honey. I'm sorry," he whispered, stroking her head with his hand. He glanced at his watch. "It's not time to get up yet. Try to go back to sleep."

He walked out across the sand, agonizing over the possibility that he had led the little girl to her death. He stopped and looked up at the stars. He wondered how the night could be so tranquil when he was so desperate.

Back at the camp, Ellie had awoken and noticed that her husband was missing. She saw his tracks in the sand and followed them with her eyes. She could barely see his figure in the darkness, but it was clear that he was down on one knee, with hands clasped and head bowed. The last time she remembered seeing him on one knee like that was when he had proposed to her. Now, she figured, he was making an entirely different proposition. She walked over to him and he glanced up at her as she approached. Without saying a word, she knelt beside him, very close, put her hands together, and bowed her head. Scott lowered his raised knee and lifted his teary face to the sky.

"No matter what happens, Lord, I thank you for giving me such a wonderful wife," Scott said aloud. Then he bowed his head and the two of them prayed together silently.

* * * * *

Molly had been unable to go back to sleep. When Scott and Ellie returned they found everyone else awake.

"You ready to hit the road?" Tom asked Scott.

"Well, I've been thinking about that," Scott replied. "That stretch of road we found definitely heads northwest. I double-checked just to make sure. I think we should ignore it and keep heading north. Any objections?"

"By the end of the day," Stoner said pessimistically, "I doubt that it will make much difference."

The group gathered their things and followed Scott into the still-dark desert. They trudged and rested, trudged and rested, across a wide, flat, low area that looked as if parts of it had been covered with water during some previous rainfall.

"It'll be dawn soon," Tom said during the third rest break.

"So?" Scott asked.

"This looks like a wadi—one of those dry river beds," Tom said. "I was just thinking that maybe we should try digging for water while it's still cool."

"We could never dig that deep," Stoner said. "When I was a boy, my crazy uncle tried to dig a well. He couldn't do it, even with a shovel and a posthole digger. Eventually he gave up and hired somebody to drill one."

"He's right, Tom," Scott said.

"Then let's get going," Tom said.

Tom led the way out of the low area, going up a long, gradual incline. Scott checked his compass to make sure they were still headed north. As they progressed up the slope, the eastern horizon began to glow. With the imminence of another scorching day, Scott began to worry about what he would do if either Stoner or Mrs. Finley collapsed. He doubted that even Tom would have the strength to carry another person. Dragging them wouldn't be much easier. Before he had decided what to do, he heard Tom's voice.

"Hey!" Tom shouted from the top of the dune, waving one arm.

Scott and Ellie started, but looked back at Stoner and the Finleys.

"Go," Stoner said. "Maybe he found something. We'll catch up."

Tom's figure disappeared as he began down the opposite side of the slope. Scott thought something might be wrong, so he increased his pace, leaving Ellie a few steps behind. If there was trouble, he wanted to face it before she did. At the top of the slope he saw it. He looked back at Ellie, then at the others. And then he, too, disappeared over the crest. When Ellie got to the top, she did the same, pausing a moment to look back before disappearing.

By the time Stoner and the Finleys got to the top, he and Mrs. Finley had to stop to catch their breath from the hurried climb. Below them, in the predawn twilight, they could see the three figures of Tom, Scott and Ellie, in single file, almost running, with about ten yards between each of them. Then a dog started to bark, and Stoner saw the village. One of those dirt-poor Bedouin villages, he assumed, but it was good enough for him.

"Tom," Scott shouted. He had been losing ground to Tom the entire time, and now Tom was nearing the village alone. Scott saw Tom slow down when the dog approached, still barking, but then a small Egyptian boy appeared. Scott could not hear what, if anything, they were saying, but after a moment he saw the boy lead Tom by the hand into the village. As he approached the village himself, people began to emerge from their homes, but he could not understand them.

"Does anyone speak English?" Scott asked, unable to think of anything else to say.

Several of the adults spoke, apparently consulting each other in Arabic. They seemed to examine Scott for a moment, then they motioned for him to walk farther into the village. As Ellie approached, another group surrounded her and brought her into the village. Scott looked back to make sure she was all right.

"Please help us," she asked her escorts, trying to make a drinking motion with her hand. "We need water. Water."

The little boy led Tom to a truck that was parked at the opposite end of the street, and the other groups followed. Two men appeared. One pulled out a key and removed a padlock from the truck's back door. He nodded to Tom and said something, but waited for Scott to get closer.

The man with the key looked Scott in the eye, then opened the back of the truck. It was filled with crates of bottled water. The two men began to break out bottles, the big one-and-a-half-liter kind, handing them to Tom and Scott and then Ellie while the crowd looked on. Tom was about to open his bottle to drink when he noticed that Scott had paused.

Scott eyed his bottle, his hand trembling a little as he held it. Never in his life had he felt such thirst and he wanted so much to drink, but instead he dropped to both knees. Tom and Ellie did the same. "Thank you, Lord," he prayed.

Then all three of them opened their bottles. They only sipped at first, but soon they were tipping their heads back and gulping the water down. As they did so, Molly ran up to them, and they saw Stoner and Mrs. Finley approaching. Scott handed Molly her own bottle, which she could barely hold, and the villagers passed bottles through the crowd to their two older guests.

And as the sun rose, its first beams struck the side of the

truck, revealing some faded lettering in both English and Arabic. The only legible English word was "relief," but the wording was accompanied by a symbol which was still clearly visible: a cross.

THE END

PARTIALITY

"Those people need to get a life," Sylvia quipped as she entered the clinic.

"How often do they protest?" Helen asked.

"You must be the new hire," Sylvia said.

"Yes, I'm Helen."

"I'm Sylvia. Nice to meet you."

"They weren't here last week when I applied," Helen noted.

"Well, you might as well get used to it," Sylvia said. "One group will protest for a week or so one month, then another group will protest for a week or two the next month."

"Are they violent?" Helen asked.

"One group threw some eggs or tomatoes or something once, a few years back," Sylvia answered. "But we've never had any real trouble."

Helen looked concerned.

"Hey, don't worry, honey," Sylvia assured her. "We've got the sheriff on our side, most of the town council, the newspaper, all kinds of national groups, and two full-time security guards."

"I've just heard so much about the death threats and the bombings at other places," Helen said.

"If it bothers you so much, why did you come to work here?" Sylvia asked.

"I lost my job at the hospital," Helen said. "And I can't afford to go without a paycheck. I have a daughter."

"Well, you've come to the right place," Sylvia said as she poured herself a cup of coffee. "You a coffee drinker?"

"No, thanks," Helen said.

"The pay's good," Sylvia continued, "and you don't have to put up with those patriarchical fascists at the hospital."

Helen just nodded, not sure how to respond.

"And Dr. Meisner is really understanding," Sylvia said. "He's very flexible with work schedules. If you need some time off, he'll let you make it up later."

"That's good to know," Helen said.

"Okay, kiddo," Sylvia said. "It's time to get started. I'll show you the ropes today. Just stick with me and take notes if you have to."

* * * * *

Helen's first week was a slow one. For four days, the clinic admitted no patients. The protesters, however, showed up each day. Helen ran the gauntlet each morning when she came in and each evening when she left. By Friday morning, she had grown used to it.

"Don't you people have anything better to do?" Helen asked as she walked between two groups of people who were chanting slogans and waving picket signs.

"They're rambunctious this morning, aren't they?" Sylvia

joked as Helen entered the building.

"They seem to be effective, too," Helen said.

"Nah," Sylvia replied. "It's not unusual for us to go a few days without a patient. But we have one today."

"Really?" Helen asked.

"Uh-huh," Sylvia said. "Harry's going to pick her up and bring her in the back way."

"Harry's the security guard?" Helen asked.

"No, Harry's our janitor," Sylvia said. "He only comes in on weekends, usually, but Meisner pays him a bonus to do special jobs."

"Oh," Helen said. "Is he the guy who sits in the back office?"

"No, that's Eddie," Sylvia explained. "He's a contractor. I'll tell you about him later."

Just then, the back door opened and Harry, dressed in a gray janitor's uniform, escorted a noticeably pregnant teenaged girl into the reception area.

"I saw protesters out front," the girl said with a Hispanic accent. "Why are they protesting?"

"Don't worry about them," Sylvia said. "Thanks, Harry."

"Let Dr. Meisner know, okay?" Harry asked as he turned to leave.

"I will," Sylvia said.

"Should I get the forms?" Helen asked.

"Yes," Sylvia said. "They're on my clipboard with the pen. Bring them into the prep room."

Helen retrieved the clipboard and followed Sylvia and the girl into the windowless preparation room. The girl sat down in the only chair.

"How much does it cost?" the girl asked.

"Do you have insurance?" Sylvia asked.

"My parents have insurance," she said, "but I don't want them to know."

"Do you have any cash?" Sylvia asked.

The girl hesitated.

"Did your boyfriend give you any money?" Sylvia asked.

"How much does it cost?" the girl asked again.

"We have special discounts for hardship cases," Sylvia said.

The girl heard the protesters singing a hymn outside.

"I don't know if I want to do this," the girl said.

"Hold on," Sylvia said, turning toward the door. "Eddie?"

As Sylvia left the room, she motioned for Helen to stay with the girl. A moment later, Helen heard Sylvia, now out of sight, speaking to Eddie in muffled tones. Eventually, Sylvia reappeared with Eddie.

"Hi, my name's Eddie," he said. "Are you Esperanza?"

"Sí, yes," she replied.

"Esperanza," Eddie began, "we offer a special program to patients in your situation. I represent a research firm that sponsors patients, like yourself, if you agree to sign a research agreement."

"What kind of research?' the girl asked.

"We're part of an international medical research community devoted to curing diseases, like Alzheimer's and Parkinson's," Eddie replied. "Esperanza, I know you're going through a tough time right now, but you can make a decision today that could potentially help millions of people. And the best part is, it won't cost you a penny."

"It's a sweet deal, honey," Sylvia added.

Esperanza, still sitting in the chair, looked up at Helen, as if seeking confirmation. Helen knew what was happening, but only turned her gaze to the floor and said nothing.

"It won't cost anything?" the girl asked after a period of silence.

"Nothing," Eddie said. "Just sign this agreement."

The girl held out her hands and Eddie handed her a pen and a clipboard with the agreement. She signed it slowly, reluctantly, but did not read it. Helen wondered if it would be legal, since the girl did not appear to be 18. As soon as the girl had signed it, Eddie took the clipboard from her.

"Don't worry," he said. "You're doing the right thing."

Then Eddie left the room. Sylvia took the other clipboard from Helen, the one with the administrative forms, and gave it to the girl.

"As soon as you fill out this paperwork," Sylvia told the girl, "we can get started."

"How long does it take?" the girl asked.

"We'll have you out of here by this afternoon," Sylvia said confidently.

"Should I get Dr. Meisner?" Helen asked.

"No, I'll get him," Sylvia said. "When she's done, put her paperwork on my desk."

"Shouldn't I file it?" Helen asked.

"No, we have a special file," Sylvia said as she stepped out of the room. "I'll explain it later."

* * * * *

In less than an hour, the girl was in the operating room and the procedure was underway. Sylvia was assisting Dr. Meisner and Helen was at the reception desk manning the phones, although none were ringing. Suddenly, a man and a woman entered through the front door with a security guard following close behind.

"I'm sorry," the guard said, "but I can't understand them, and I don't think they can understand me."

The man and the woman were clearly upset and both were speaking, almost shouting, in Spanish.

"No hablo español," Helen said. "No hablo español."

Helen motioned with her hands for the couple to stay and then went to the operating room. She opened the operating room door just enough to poke her head in.

"I'm sorry Dr. Meisner," Helen said, "but I think the girl's parents are here."

"What do you mean you 'think?'" Meisner asked, not looking up from his work.

"They're very upset and they're yelling at me in Spanish," Helen answered. "What do I do?"

"I know a little Spanish," Sylvia said. "Helen, stay here and assist. I won't be long, Dr. Meisner."

"Okay," Meisner said, "but make it quick."

Helen stood next to the counter just inside the door. She was glad that she did not have a clear view of the doctor's work, although she was not sure why she felt that way.

"I thought everyone spoke Spanish these days," Meisner said as he continued to work.

"I took Latin," Helen replied.

"Latin?" Meisner said. "I hope you're not Catholic."

"No," Helen said. "I'm...not...."

"Uh-oh," Meisner said, referring to his work.

"What's wrong?" Helen asked.

"I can't..." he started. "Can you help me here?"

Helen started toward him but clumsily bumped into the instrument cart. She stopped when she saw what was happening. Two small legs were out, and Meisner was having trouble holding them and his instruments at the same time.

Then, without warning, Helen heard a slight thud.

"Crap," Meisner blurted out. "I need some help here."

Helen inched closer. The entire head had emerged. It looked to Helen as if Meisner were trying to push the head back in, but he was having no success. Before she could do or say anything, Meisner plunged his blade into the skull.

"Sylvia!" he cried out. "Sylvia, get in here!"

Helen could not believe it. She gasped and covered her mouth with both hands. She instinctively backed up, crashing into the instrument cart again. As she did so, Sylvia came through the door.

"What's wrong?" Sylvia asked.

"I need suction," Meisner said angrily.

Sylvia rushed to help, glancing disparagingly at Helen.

As the suction began, Helen could see the tissue matter start to flow through the clear tube. In shock, she sank to the floor, with her back against a cabinet door and her eyes glazed over.

When it was finished, Eddie came in, wearing surgical gloves. Sylvia put the little body on a cold metal tray and handed it to him, and he left without saying a word.

"Buck up, kiddo," Sylvia said, using her foot to tap Helen on the leg. "Stuff like this happens every now and then. It's not your fault."

"Helen, uh, why don't you take the rest of the day off?" Meisner suggested nervously. "Paid leave, of course. Sylvia and I can finish up here."

By this time, Sylvia had removed her surgical gloves and washed her hands. She reached down and pulled Helen up by the arm.

"Never turn down time off with pay," Sylvia said.

Helen just shook her head, still in shock. Sylvia led her

out of the operating room and told her to go home. As Helen walked to the reception desk to get her purse, she could see the girl's parents sitting in the lobby. They stared at her but said nothing. A moment later, when she walked out of the front door, the protesters rose to their feet and shouted at her as they usually did, but this time she actually listened to what they were saying.

"Baby killer," some said derisively.

"Stop the slaughter!" others chanted.

One of them pushed his way through the crowd to the police tape that separated the protesters from the sidewalk and asked "When did you first receive your body, huh? When was your DNA first created? When did your body's metabolism begin? At conception. A human being's life begins at conception."

She glanced at him as she walked past, too confused to respond. But amid the shouts she heard another voice, a gentle voice.

"Are you all right?" the voice asked.

She turned to see an elderly man standing among the protesters. She stopped walking and stared at him.

"Are you all right?" he asked again.

"No," Helen said.

"Can I help?" he asked.

"I don't know," she said.

The other protesters began to see that something was happening and they grew silent. The elderly man, in violation of the law, ducked under the police tape and approached Helen. He took her gently by the arm and led her down the sidewalk to the parking lot.

"Would you like to go somewhere and talk?" he asked.

"Are you a priest?" Helen asked. "Because I'm not

religious…."

"No," he said.

"I…" Helen started. "I haven't had lunch."

"There's a little sandwich place around the corner," the man suggested. "Good french fries."

"Okay," Helen agreed.

* * * * *

In the dim, pub-like restaurant, the man asked for the corner booth along the back wall. Its tall, cushioned seats made it the quietest spot in the place, and its more isolated location offered some privacy from the other customers. The short walk and the pub's hushed atmosphere had helped Helen regain her composure. After ordering some sandwiches, the unlikely pair resumed their conversation.

"My name's Paul, by the way," the man said.

"I'm Helen."

"So, what happened in there today?" Paul asked.

"I don't know," Helen said softly, looking down to avoid Paul's gaze.

"It must have been something," Paul said.

"If you're not a priest," Helen said, deliberately changing the subject, "what are you?"

"I'm a Christian," Paul said, smiling a bit and allowing the subject to be changed. "I'm also a retired insurance salesman."

"I'm a nurse," Helen said, almost smiling a bit herself.

The waitress interrupted them for a moment, putting their drinks on the table, but left quickly.

"So how did you become a Christian?" Helen asked, glad to get her mind off of the day's earlier events.

"Well, I guess you could say I took the intellectual approach," Paul answered.

"How do you mean?" Helen asked.

"Some people are born into Christian families," Paul said. "Others attend a church service or revival meeting and experience some sort of emotional conversion."

"But not you?" Helen surmised.

"Not me," Paul said. "I didn't really think about the big questions until college. Eventually I decided on Christianity."

"What big questions?" Helen asked.

"Oh, you know," Paul said. "Does God exist? What is the purpose of existence? Stuff like that."

"What is the meaning of life, basically," Helen said.

"Well, not quite," Paul said. "If you ask 'what is the meaning of life?' some smart aleck will probably say something like 'any organic or carbon-based entity with DNA and a metabolism.' I think that what people really mean when they ask that question is 'what is the purpose of existence?' "

"Whose existence?" Helen asked.

"My existence," Paul said, "your existence, the existence of mankind, the existence of life, the existence of the universe. All existence, really."

"So, for you," Helen said, "the big question is 'what is the purpose of existence?' "

"That and 'does God exist?' " Paul replied.

"*Does* God exist?" Helen asked.

"Well, I think before you can answer that question you have to decide whether anything exists at all," Paul said. "Does the universe really exist?"

"What do you mean by that?" Helen asked.

"In college," Paul said, " I learned about this philosopher who said 'I think, therefore, I am."

"Cogito ergo sum," Helen said, translating the famous phrase into its original Latin.

"That's right," Paul said. "The point was that we cannot really trust our senses. Everything we see, everything we hear or taste or smell or touch, could all be just an illusion. The philosopher decided that the only thing he could know for sure, with absolute certainty, was that he existed."

"Because if he could think to ask the question," Helen said, "then he himself must exist."

"Right," Paul said. "But I kept thinking about it even after the semester was over. I eventually decided that not only do I exist, but other things must exist, too."

"Why?" Helen asked.

"Simply because there are things that I do not know and things which I cannot control," Paul said. "Therefore, not only do I exist because I think, but something other than me must also exist."

Just then, the waitress arrived with their sandwiches.

"So the universe does exist," Helen concluded, glancing at the sandwiches and then at Paul.

The waitress, having heard only Helen's last statement, raised a questioning eyebrow, but then smiled and walked away.

"Yes," Paul said after the waitress had left, "the universe does exist. Of course, not everyone agrees on what the universe is."

"It's everything, isn't it?" Helen asked.

"But what is everything?" Paul responded. "Some people, for example, say that the universe is a material, four dimensional, space-time continuum and nothing else. They don't believe in an afterlife or any kind of spiritual existence. Other people say that only the mind exists and that all material substance is just an illusion."

"What do they mean by that?" Helen asked.

"Well, for one thing," Paul said, "it means that either I am just a figment of your imagination, or you are just a figment of my imagination."

"Okay, I get it," Helen said.

"Some interpretations of the one-mind school also include the idea that each person is somehow a god," Paul said, "or at least that we each create our own reality."

"Sort of a New Age thing, huh?" Helen commented.

"There is also a third school of thought concerning the nature of the universe," Paul continued. "Advocates of this school believe that the material, four dimensional, space-time continuum exists, but that there is also a spiritual realm. In other words, the third school allows for the possibility of souls, an afterlife and the existence of one or more supernatural gods."

"For a retired insurance salesman," Helen said, "you're quite the philosopher. So which school is right?"

"I ruled out the one-giant-mind idea right away," Paul said. "Like I said before, if there are things that I do not know, and things that I cannot do, then how could my mind possibly be the only thing that exists? And if I'm a god, or if I 'create my own reality,' then how come I still get stuck in traffic?"

"Good point," Helen agreed.

"So it came down to a battle between the materialists and the spiritual afterlife types," Paul said. "And when I say 'spiritualist,' I'm not talking only about psychics and astrologers and people like that. I mean everyone who believes that the universe includes some sort of spiritual realm in addition to the space-time continuum."

"I'm with you," Helen said.

"I figured that if I could prove or disprove the existence of God," Paul said, "then that would determine which school was right. But a friend of mine in college disagreed. He said that God could exist in the materialist universe with no afterlife and no souls. At first I objected, but he explained that God could be thought of simply as an impersonal natural force, the ultimate physical cause of the entire universe. Sort of like gravity or electromagnetism, only greater."

"So your friend was looking at the universe as if it were just some giant 'cause-and-effect' scientific experiment?" Helen wondered.

"Yes, exactly," Paul said. "In fact, he and I both agreed that, because science is based on the study of cause and effect, God has to exist."

"As the cause of the universe?" Helen asked.

"Yes," Paul said.

"You make it sound so simple," Helen said skeptically.

"Look around," Paul said. "Look at the world, the people, the stars at night. Where does it all come from? Why does it all exist? Sure, the actual physics might be beyond our comprehension, but is the idea of a Creator really so far-fetched?"

"Well…" Helen started.

"Everything that exists has a cause, or multiple causes," Paul continued. "And every event that occurs has a cause, or multiple causes. And this holds true at the subatomic level, the atomic level, the molecular level, the organic tissue level, the human and animal entity level, and even at the planetary or astronomical level. No matter where we look, cause and effect holds true. So, if you think of the universe as a single entity, as a single "effect," then it must have a single cause."

"And that cause is God?" Helen asked in conclusion.

"Yes," Paul said.

"So why can't there be two gods?" Helen asked. "Or lots of gods?"

"Well," Paul began, "taken to its logical conclusion, the principle of cause and effect suggests that there must be a single, ultimate source for everything that exists. Therefore, multiple inferior gods or supernatural beings might exist, but they cannot be the ultimate source of the universe because they cannot be, in and of themselves, the cause of their own plurality."

"So you're not ruling out the possibility of demigods," Helen asked, "you're just saying that, ultimately, if demigods do exist, then they must have a Creator, too?"

"Uhh…I prefer to think more along the line of angels," Paul said, "rather than demigods. But basically, if there's more than one of something, then there must be a *reason* that there's more than one."

"Interesting," Helen said, "but does plurality really require a cause?"

"Well, look," Paul said, "I'm not saying that this is a mathematical proof. It's just a line of reasoning but, taken as whole, I think it is the most plausible of all possible arguments."

"But there must be more to it," Helen said.

"There is," Paul said. "My friend and I decided that the next step was to determine whether God is just an impersonal, physical force, or if God is a personal, spiritual God."

"It sounds like your friend was just as interested in this as you were," Helen said.

"Actually, I didn't know it at the time, but my friend was

a Christian," Paul said. "He was a physics major, though, so I had assumed back then that he was one of those secular humanist scientists. I was surprised when I found out that he was a Christian."

"So I guess he was pushing the concept of a personal God?" Helen asked.

"Yes, but he was very objective about it," Paul said. "I think he was going through a period of doubt. I guess all those left-wing professors and textbooks were really putting his faith to the test."

"I assume he convinced you, though?" Helen asked.

"Not really," Paul said. "We went our separate ways and I ended up deciding in favor of a personal God on my own."

"How did you do that?" Helen asked.

"I thought about it and I thought about it," Paul said. "Finally, it struck me. How could an impersonal God create a universe that included conscious, sentient, moral beings, without being a conscious, sentient and moral being himself?"

For the first time in the conversation, Helen said nothing. She just looked at Paul, and he was not sure how to take it.

"I guess that's not a good enough argument for most people…" Paul started.

"No," Helen said contemplatively. "No, I think you're right. I think that's a very good argument. God exists because cause and effect requires that the universe have an ultimate cause. And God is a personal God, because his creation includes personal beings."

"I like to think that that's what the Bible means when it says that God created us in his image," Paul said.

"You mean he made us sentient, moral beings because he's a sentient, moral being?" Helen asked. "Isn't that getting into a circular argument?"

"Maybe," Paul said. "But the Bible also says that God is the Alpha and the Omega, the beginning and the end."

"Those are the first and last letters of the Greek alphabet, right?" Helen asked.

"Yes," Paul said. "But the whole concept fits right in with God being the cause of the universe. He's the beginning or 'Alpha' because he created everything, and he's the end or 'Omega' because he is the ultimate purpose of existence."

"You mean the purpose of *our* existence?" Helen asked.

"The purpose of everything," Paul said, "including the purpose of our existence. If God does not exist, then there is no ultimate purpose of existence. But how could there not be a purpose of existence?"

"So God must exist if existence itself is to have any real meaning or purpose," Helen concluded.

"Exactly," Paul said. "The purpose of existence and the existence of God are inextricably linked. You cannot determine one without determining the other."

"Are you sure you're not a retired quantum physicist?" Helen joked. "But I still want to know the purpose of *our* existence. What is the ultimate purpose for the existence of humanity?"

"Ultimately, it's to love and glorify God," Paul said, "although I also assume that God has a unique plan for each individual."

"To love and glorify God?" Helen asked.

"If God is the creator of the universe," Paul said, "the creator of all that exists, then he deserves all of the glory, don't you think?"

"But if that's true," Helen said, noticeably more somber, "then ultimately he also deserves all of the blame, too."

"The blame?" Paul asked.

"The blame for all of the suffering in the world," Helen said. "What I am trying to say is, if God created us, and if he really is omnipotent and omniscient, then isn't he ultimately responsible for our flaws and shortcomings? He must have known when he made us that we would not be perfect, so shouldn't he accept responsibility?"

Paul put both elbows on the table and slowly rubbed is palms together, contemplating how he would respond. He looked down for a moment and then looked back up at Helen, lowering his hands.

"I know of one religion," he began, "that says God deserves all of the glory *and* that he accepts the blame for all of mankind's sins. It's not that God is directly responsible for our sins, because each of us is a moral being with free will, but God does accept ultimate responsibility."

Then the idea began to take root in Helen's mind, and Paul could see it in her face.

"Is that..." she stammered. "Is that what Christians mean when they say...."

She could not quite finish the thought.

"Yes," Paul said. "That's why Christ died on the cross: to accept the blame for our sins. And he has the power, the authority, to accept that blame because he is God, because he did create us, because he is the ultimate source of all that exists. He didn't *have* to do it, but he wanted to because he loves us."

Helen hesitated for a moment. She had not expected this.

"Is it really true?" she asked. "Can it really be true?"

"I believe it is," Paul said.

"Excuse me," Helen said as she got up to go to the ladies' room.

* * * * *

When Helen returned to the table, it was obvious to Paul that she had been crying.

"If there really is a God…" she started to ask, but stopped. "Well, I don't want to take up your whole afternoon."

"I'm retired," Paul said. "And I can't think of a better way to spend the afternoon."

"If there really is a God, why does he allow so much suffering?" she asked.

It was an age-old question, but Paul sensed that for Helen, it had some great personal significance.

"Some say that God allows us to suffer to build our character," Paul started.

"How does getting tortured to death build one's character?" Helen said brusquely, cutting him off. "How does getting killed by a tornado build one's character?"

"Some questions have more than one answer," Paul said. "Sometimes, suffering builds character or teaches us an important lesson, like a child burning his finger on a hot stove. He suffers a little in the short term, but he'll be wiser for it in the long term."

"Okay, fair enough," Helen said, somewhat calmer.

"But the existence of suffering also has a broader effect," Paul continued. "The existence of suffering proves that life is serious. It proves that life is not the equivalent of some video game. In other words, the existence of suffering proves that our actions have moral consequences, and that the moral choices we make are important."

"So the nihilists are wrong when they claim that nothing really matters?" Helen asked.

"The nihilists are wrong," Paul answered. "Life matters.

Morality matters. What you believe and how you behave will have serious consequences, for yourself and for others. The existence of suffering proves it."

"But some suffering is caused by accident," Helen said, now more subdued, "or by natural forces."

"True," Paul said. "People can suffer because of natural disasters, accidents or malicious intent. The bottom line is, we have all suffered in one way or another, and that is how we know that it is wrong to cause others to suffer."

"Then why do people inflict so much suffering on each other?" Helen asked. "Why must the world be so...."

"Fallen?" Paul asked.

"Fallen?" Helen echoed. "What do you mean?"

"I'm referring to the fall from grace," Paul answered. "You know the story. Original sin. Adam and Eve. The serpent and the forbidden fruit. We got kicked out of the Garden of Eden because of our disobedience. Now here we are, depraved individuals with lots of free will, living in a fallen world, tempted by evil at every turn. No wonder suffering exists."

"So why doesn't God put an end to it?" Helen asked.

"Because he's merciful," Paul said.

"Merciful?" Helen objected. "Since when does allowing suffering count as mercy?"

"To end suffering," Paul answered, "God would have to destroy us all, wouldn't he? How could God be a just God if he let our disobedience go unpunished? Remember Noah and the Flood? Remember Sodom and Gomorrah? Then again, perhaps he could just take away our free will; turn us into robots or something. But I don't think God wants to destroy us, and I don't think he wants us to be robots, either. If he did, he would have made robots in the first place, instead of human beings with free will."

"So what does he want?" Helen asked.

"I think he wants us to freely choose to love him," Paul said. "Look, I know the robot thing is a cliché, but to love is a choice that can only be made by a being with free will. He wants us to love him. And to love each other, by the way."

"Does Christianity teach that?" Helen asked.

"Christ himself taught that the greatest commandment is to love God," Paul said. "And that the second greatest commandment is to love your neighbor as yourself. These summarize the Ten Commandments found in the Old Testament."

"But we don't do that," Helen said.

"Not like we should," Paul said. "People are sinners."

"You mean non-Christians are sinners?" Helen asked.

"No," Paul answered. "That's a common misconception. Christians believe that all people have sinned in one way or another, including Christians themselves."

"But what does that mean?" Helen asked.

"Well, for one thing," Paul began, "it means that we're not merely imperfect, but depraved. We don't just make mistakes by accident; we actually do things that are wrong *deliberately*, even when we know that they're wrong. I know from my own experience that I'm a sinner. I think things that I know are wrong, I speak things that I know are wrong and I do things that I know are wrong. I wish that I were not a sinner, but at least I acknowledge it. A lot of people don't want to admit it."

"Why should they?" Helen asked. "Why admit it if you can't do anything about it? Don't get me wrong. I think you're right. I think human nature is depraved. I've seen things…I've done things myself…but we can't change human nature."

"No, we can't," Paul said. "We are going to be disobedient to God because of our sinful natures. And, I suppose, because we are born into a sinful world. And that means that we are going to suffer."

"So there's no hope?" Helen asked. "We all have to suffer just because Adam and Eve sinned? That doesn't seem fair."

"You're forgetting the good part," Paul said. "Or the good *news*, I should say. God confined himself to the form of a man and suffered the penalty for our sins, so that we might be reconciled to him. He suffered so that our suffering can end, at least when we go to live with him in heaven. All we have to do is accept his sacrifice. That's what becoming a Christian is all about. You admit that you are a sinner, that you can't do anything about it on your own, and you accept God's forgiveness. You accept that Christ died for you, to pay the price for your sins. You get to keep your free will in this life and you get to go to heaven in the next. That's more than fair, don't you think?"

"You make it all seem to fit together so well," Helen said haltingly.

"Like we said before, God *must* exist because the universe must have a reason for existing," Paul reminded her. "And God must be a *personal* God because his creation includes personal beings. And surely our depravity and our suffering indicate that something has gone wrong between us and God. And surely Christ is the means of reconciliation, for what else would God say to us, if not what Christ said? Love God, love your neighbor, love your enemies. What a world that would be...."

"You really believe it, don't you?" Helen asked.

"What else can I believe?" Paul admitted. "Atheism provides no answers. Agnosticism provides no answers.

Paganism is patently absurd. Think about it: without God, life is pointless; without Christ, life is hopeless. Christianity really is the best explanation for why we are here. It explains the origins of the universe. It explains the purpose of existence. It explains why people are so depraved. And best of all, it tells us how to get right with God."

"And how is that?" Helen asked.

"We need to pray to God and accept Christ as our savior," Paul answered. "Tell God that, even though you might not understand it all, you're willing to take a leap of faith and put your trust in him. Admit to him that you're a sinner. Tell him that you're sorry for your sins and ask for his forgiveness. Tell him that you'd like to be born again, like it says in the Bible, and then ask Jesus to come into your heart. Ask for his help and guidance, and be sure to thank him."

Helen took a deep breath but said nothing.

"A prayer like that is sometimes called the Sinner's Prayer," Paul continued, "although the wording can vary. After you pray it, you should look for a good church and eventually get baptized. Some people go to church first and say the prayer with the pastor or a friend. If you like, you can come to my church this Sunday."

Helen looked at Paul for a moment before speaking, flattered that he would care enough to make such a proposal. She was not sure what to say.

"I've never really thought about all of this," she eventually replied. "Not all at one time, anyway. I've always thought that Christians were…."

"Ignorant fools?" Paul said with a grin. "Intolerant bigots?"

"Well, yeah," Helen admitted.

"Don't feel bad," Paul said. "I used to think that way, too."

When they had finished their sandwiches, Paul paid the

waitress and Helen accepted his offer to walk her to her car.

* * * * *

Upon arriving at her car in the parking lot, just across the street from the clinic, Helen pulled out her keys but turned to Paul before unlocking the car door.

"Thank you for lunch," she said.

"You're very welcome," Paul said, handing her one of his old business cards so that she would have his phone number. "But I have a confession to make. I've actually been hoping to have a conservation like this. Not necessarily with you or anyone in particular, but, well, you know."

"So you've been practicing?" Helen guessed.

"Well, sort of," Paul said, "but you can only get so far intellectually."

"What do you mean?" Helen asked.

"Eventually," he said, "you have to take that leap of faith. You have to pray the Sinner's Prayer."

"I'm not sure I'm ready for that," Helen said, "but I will think about what you've said."

"Will you do me a favor?" Paul asked.

"What?" Helen asked.

"Do you have a copy of the Bible at home?" Paul asked.

"Yes," Helen said.

"Read the Gospel of John," Paul said, "in the New Testament. Even if you don't understand all of it, I think it's important to read the word of God."

"Okay, I will," Helen said, "as a special favor to my favorite insurance salesman."

"*Retired* salesman," Paul corrected her.

"No," Helen said, smiling. "I don't think you ever retired.

I think you just found a different underwriter."

Paul returned her smile and stepped back as Helen got into her car and rolled her window down.

"I really enjoyed talking to you," Paul said, hoping that he had helped.

"Me, too," Helen said.

With that, she drove off.

* * * * *

The following Monday, after calling Meisner to submit her verbal resignation, Helen drove downtown to the district police station. Once inside, she approached a uniformed officer but, before she could speak, he pointed to the central desk in the middle of the lobby. She approached the officer behind the desk, outwardly confident but trembling inside.

"Excuse me," she said.

"Yes?" the officer said, looking up from the computer.

"I'd like to report a crime," Helen said.

"What kind of crime?" the officer asked flatly.

Helen paused, but only for a brief moment.

"A murder."

THE END